THE GATES
OF
PARADISE

William Blake, one who is very much delighted with
being in good Company. Born Novr 1757 in London
and has died several times since.
Written by Blake, 16 January 1826

Peter Carter

THE GATES
OF
PARADISE

Illustrated by
Fermin Rocker

London
OXFORD UNIVERSITY PRESS
1974

Oxford University Press, Ely House, London W.1
GLASGOW NEW YORK TORONTO MELBOURNE WELLINGTON
CAPE TOWN IBADAN NAIROBI DAR ES SALAAM LUSAKA ADDIS ABABA
DELHI BOMBAY CALCUTTA MADRAS KARACHI LAHORE DACCA
KUALA LUMPUR SINGAPORE HONG KONG TOKYO

ISBN 0 19 271367 1

© Peter Carter 1974
First published 1974

Printed in Great Britain by
Lowe & Brydone (Printers) Ltd.,
London and Thetford

Preface

This book is a sketch of a great poet during a brief period of his life. The details concerning Blake, his wife, and his friends are factual. The rest is fiction, but that can be true in its own way.

After a lifetime spent in penury and obscurity, William Blake died in London at six o'clock on the afternoon of 12 August 1827, listening to music.

Chapter 1

In the Year of Grace 1796, William Blake walked in his garden. The autumn dew sparkled on his vine and the hedge was clouded white with gossamer. The sun shone, and insects, feeling its warmth, flew from the rhubarb bed, visible only by the light glinting from their wings.

William saw these things and rejoiced in them. And he saw his apple-tree and his medlar-tree with the clothes-line stretched between them, and the washing on the line which made him think of the blissful souls which flew over the streets of Lambeth. And he saw the prophet Isaiah, his face radiant with glory, robed in blue flames, walking barefoot through the grass. Beyond his hedge he saw the Lunatic Asylum, silent in its misery, and, through a hole in the hedge, he thought he saw a boy peering at him.

Deep in thought, he walked back to his house. Isaiah he often saw, and other prophets, ghosts, and spirits, too, but he had never before seen a boy looking at him through the hedge. He asked his wife, Sophy, whether she could see the boy. Sophy looked through the window and said that there was no one there. Then William knew that the boy was a vision.

He thought about this, wondering why the vision had come to him, and what it might mean. He wondered if it could be his dead brother, Robert. He did not recognize the face, but he allowed that spirits could assume their own shapes. Then he dismissed the idea. He had spoken to Robert only three days previously. Finally he stopped thinking about the matter, the spirit would tell him who it was in its own time.

He rose and went into his work-room. William was an engraver. His skill was to cut pictures into copper plate so that they could be reproduced. Sometimes he drew his own work, but more often, in order to live, he had to copy other men's. Copying he hated; it was bondage, drudgery, especially such a picture as he was engraving now: a languid girl fondling a puppy . . . roses . . . simpers. He shook his head in disgust: disgust that he should have to labour over it, that another man should have drawn it, that other men should buy it. He opened his notebook, which he kept by him, and wrote in it: 'If you wish to degrade mankind, first degrade Art.'

He repeated the phrase to himself once or twice, then turned to his work. The copper plate he was engraving was mounted on a wheel set horizontally in his bench, with the original picture by it. The work was half-done. Across the plate ran a network of lines but its centre was clear, a tranquil pool, unruffled, undisturbed.

William looked into this pool. Deep in its burnished depths he saw the reflection of his face, his red hair redder still, his pale skin as swarthy as an Indian's. Many a man, seeing his face, will look at it, wondering about the mysteries which lie beneath the skin and bone; but William looked beyond his reflection, down into the bottom of the pool of light. There he saw shapes, lights rather than shapes, which flickered and shimmered like snakes in a lake burnished by a tropical sun.

For a long time William looked into the copper. As he looked, it was as if, for him, the light drained from the bright morning sky, and shadows, blacker than the plumes of mourners, crept into the corners of the room. The lights in the copper flickered, fawn and red and green, and William saw a dark sky there, streaked with golden fires and fretted with fronds — darker yet, which moved and trembled as if

2

some great striped body slid through them. Lost in his vision he thought he heard the vibrating roar of an untrammelled animal.

But although the world was lost to William, he was not lost to it. He was being watched. For Sophy had been wrong. There was a boy in the garden.

The boy was called Ben. Three days before, he had run away from a candle-maker in Spitalfields, and since then he had been skulking among the gardens of Lambeth, living on roots and grass like an animal. He did not look human. His face was stained red and blue with the juice of berries, he was encrusted with grease and tallow, and grass and leaves stuck to him. But hunger and cold were driving him back to his own species. In the kitchen in the house at the bottom of the garden was a blue and white jug. Ben was sure it contained milk. But in the next window was a man with his head in his hands. Ben knew the man by sight. He had seen him walking in the garden, nodding and bowing, and talking when there was no one else there. Ben was desperate with hunger but he was afraid of the man. Had it not been for him Ben might have gone to the woman who lived in the house and asked her for food. But the woman had gone out, the man seemed to be asleep, and Ben needed the food. Shaking with fear he began to crawl down the garden.

As if in a dream William heard the growl of an animal and smelt the rank odour of something wild. He opened his eyes. A shape was moving down the garden: a vague, blurred shape, covered with the debris of the earth, crawling like an animal, and yet not like an animal, and with something indistinctly human about its piebald face. Unmoving, William watched it creep along the hedge until it came under his window. Then, with joy in his heart, he rose and leaned forward.

'Hail, Spirit of the Earth!' he cried.

Chapter 2

Sophy came round the corner of the house, her basket on her arm, to find William beaming through the window.

'Do you see this spectre, my dear?' he asked, his face aglow with delight.

Sophy peered closely at Ben. William saw things no other man saw, saw them so clearly, and with such force, that she herself saw them, or nearly. But, eager though she was to see spectres, she was in no doubt about the terror-stricken figure before her.

'It is a boy, William,' she said.

'Oh!' William leaned through the window and prodded Ben. 'Oh, what is a boy doing in our garden?'

'I don't know.' Sophy turned to Ben. 'What do you want?'

Ben hardly knew what he wanted any more. He was so frightened he could not move, otherwise he would have run away.

'He may be hungry,' Sophy said.

Since it had turned out that his discovery was not a creature born of the elements, William's interest had ebbed away, but if the boy was hungry he should have food. He led the way to the kitchen. There, Sophy poured out milk from the blue-and-white jug and cut a slice of bread. Ben drank and ate, his eyes flicking from Sophy to William.

'He's like a condemned man eating his last meal,' Sophy said. 'What is your name, boy?'

Ben stood on one leg, writhing with embarrassment. 'Ben,' he blurted out, spitting bread over the table.

'Ben what?'

'Ben Pendrill.'

'I have never heard of a name like that before,' Sophy said. 'How have you come to get so black? I have never seen anyone so dirty in my life.'

Ben shuffled his feet and looked at the floor. Sophy sighed.

'Well, if you have had enough to eat you had better be

4

getting off home. Your mother will be wondering where you are. Where do you live?'

Again Ben was silent. The task of explaining himself to this large, soft-spoken woman, and the silent, pale-faced man, was utterly beyond him. He wriggled and a few leaves detached themselves from him and fell to the floor. As if this was his cue, William spoke.

'Perhaps he has no mother. Perhaps he has no father, nor home either.'

'Is that so, boy?' Sophy asked.

Ben nodded.

'Oh!' Sophy was distressed. 'It is true, William. He has nothing, neither parents nor home.'

'Then he is a free spirit,' William answered. 'He has an untrammelled soul with nought to clog him nor bind him.'

'That is so.' Sophy was deeply moved by William's words. She thought of a bird, soaring on white pinions in a cloudless sky. Then she looked at Ben, wretched in his filthiness.

'But he needs a home,' she said. 'Even birds have nests. And he must eat, and he needs washing.'

She turned, anxious for William's approval, but he had gone. He had left the room as soundlessly as a ghost. If Sophy was startled she gave no sign of it. She rolled up her sleeves briskly.

'Whatever happens to you, boy,' she said, 'you won't leave my house dirty.'

There was a boiling-copper in the kitchen. Sophy filled it with water, swinging the heavy bucket up as easily as a man. She knelt and blew the fire beneath until it glowed into a red heat, roaring as it sucked in the air.

'That won't take long to boil,' Sophy said. 'Now, let's have those clothes of yours. Wrap this round you.'

She gave Ben a sheet and took his clothes as he reluctantly handed them over. She stuffed the rags in the copper and began scouring Ben. As she worked she tutted in amazement.

Ben's head was being joggled so violently that he could hardly speak but a spark of rebellion was kindled by the sudden attack on him.

'It's the tallow,' he shouted. 'When we boiled up the tallow it splashed all over us, and we got it on us when we made the candles.'

'Oh, so that's what you are, is it?' Sophy said. 'A candle-maker. And what are you doing round Lambeth?'

Suddenly shy, Ben fell silent, but Sophy, who could draw wild sparrows to her, coaxed his story from him.

'It was old Carlin what used to have us boiling the tallow. He used to bash us when he was drunk.'

'He struck you?' Sophy was shocked.

'Yes, Ma, and he kicked us too.' Ben squinted at Sophy's gentle face and had a burst of inspiration. 'And he got little kids and stuck 'em in the boiler for to make candles of them. And he was going to do it to me, so I ran away.'

By now Sophy had cleaned away a good deal of the filth from Ben's face which gleamed unnaturally white against the blackness of his body.

'You don't have a bad face, now I can see it,' she said. 'But is that true about boiling you into candles? I wouldn't like to believe that about any man. Beating and kicking is bad enough, but did he really do that? Did he make candles out of boys?'

Ben went red and turned his face away, but Sophy held his chin and turned him back.

'No, it's not true, is it? William wouldn't like to hear you telling lies.'

'Who's he?' Ben demanded.

'He is my husband,' Sophy said.

'And what's your name, Ma?'

'Why, I have two names,' Sophy said. 'Catherine Sophia. Most like to call me Catherine, but William always calls me Sophy. Catherine, now, she was a woman that was burned to death on a wheel by wicked men. You've seen a Catherine-Wheel, haven't you, on Guy Fawkes Night, when they have the bonfires?'

'Yes.' Ben scrubbed his head with a towel. 'What does that other name mean, the one your governor likes?'

Sophy blushed. 'Oh that. It's a Greek word. It means wisdom, Heavenly Wisdom. William told me that. I never knew what it meant until he told me. Here. . .' She opened the copper and stirred vigorously in its depths with a stick. 'These clothes are boiled away, nearly.' She dragged a mangle from a corner. 'You can turn the handle while I twist the clothes in.'

Ben took hold of the handle and gave a tug. The rollers crept round grudgingly. Sophy pulled Ben away and spun the handle, feeding the clothes into the roller.

'You're good at that, Ma,' Ben cried.

Sophy laughed. 'Why, when I was a girl I could turn a handle from morning till night.' She began to sing, in a light sweet voice:

> ' 'Twas on a Monday morning-O,
> When I beheld my Darling-O,
> She looked so sweet and nimble-O,
> In every high degree.

'Do you know that song, Ben? Why, all the girls sing it when they are washing. But there's more to it than just scrubbing. You have to bleach and starch and iron, yes. . .'

Easily she swung the handle and the huge wooden rollers gobbled up Ben's shirt and trousers.

'Do you see that, Ben? When I was young I used to think that the mangle was like a face eating up the clothes, and the tub behind was its belly. Folk laughed at me when I told them that, but William didn't laugh. He said that I had the soul of a poet and he kissed me for it.'

She sang again and Ben, although he did not know the words, found his mouth opening with sympathy.

> 'She looked so sweet and nimble-O,
> A-washing of her linen-O,
> Dashing away with the smoothing iron
> She stole my heart away.'

Ben was to remember that moment for a long time: the steam, the smell of the soap, the rumble of the mangle, and the singing of the woman whose name meant Holy Wisdom.

Sophy hung the clothes before the fire and sat down. Ben, muffled in a sheet, sat, too.

'What does he do, then, your governor?' he asked.

'William?' Even Ben could see the glow which shone from Sophy's face when William was mentioned.

'Why, he is a poet and an artist.'

Ben had no idea what a poet was and wanted to know.

Sophy leaned forward and rearranged Ben's clothes on the fireguard. 'That is a man who sees what no other man sees, and says it in words no other man has used. I will show you.'

She ran from the room and came back with a book. 'Here, these are some of William's poems and pictures.'

Ben took the book and stared at it blankly. Sophy leaned

7

forward and her face fell.

'You have it upside down!'

Ben stooped, his face white and miserable, and Sophy bit her lip.

'Oh,' she said. 'You can't read. Well then, you are like I was before I met William. I didn't know my letters no more than that mangle does, and I was twenty! Why, when I married I had to put a cross on the register! But William taught me. Yes, he taught me how to read and write when all I was good for was the washing. Now I can read as well as the Queen. I'll teach you, if you like.'

She sat on a chair and pulled Ben to her. 'I helped to make this book. Do you see these pictures? William drew them and there have been none like them in the history of the world. William learnt how to print them in. . .' She stopped abruptly and put her hand to her breast. 'I'll not tell you that now. Do you see this page?'

But Ben was not looking at the book, he was staring over her shoulder at the pale-faced man with red hair and blue eyes who had appeared so silently.

Sophy turned, too, and placed the book in her lap. 'William,' she said, 'I was teaching Ben how to read.'

William gazed at them both, his eyes wide as a cat's. 'Does he wish it?'

'Well.' Sophy was flustered. 'I think he must.'

William shook his head. 'There is no must. If his desires are to be perfect they will grow from him. We are not gardeners to plant the seed of obedience.'

William's rebuke was mild, but Sophy felt it keenly. She fingered the book. 'Is Ben to stay with us, then?'

'We have food,' William said. 'We have a roof over our heads. He may stay with us until his spirit wills otherwise.'

Chapter 3

It took Ben a long time to get to sleep that night. He was uncomfortable in his cleanliness and the smell of washed linen disturbed him. He was afraid of William and his fears were not stilled when candle-light glimmered under his door and, peering through the jamb, Ben saw him pacing the corridor, his lips moving in communion with some invisible being. More than once he thought of running away, but sleep claimed him for its own.

When he woke the weather had broken. The garden was shrouded with mist and the leaves of the vine, which climbed across the window, shimmered with water. Still in a shirt of William's which had done duty for a nightgown, he stole down the stairs.

The house was quiet. A clock with a ship painted on it ticked away slowly, but there was no other sound. He went into the parlour but there was no one there. The kitchen was empty, too, save for a cat purring before the fire. As Ben entered the room it gave a throaty 'churrup' and slipped out of the door.

Ben tiptoed down the hallway. There was a door at the end. He paused by it and listened. There was no sound. He slid the door open and looked around it. William and Sophy were there, sitting opposite each other at a bench, he in white linen, she in a robe of blue. Both of them were motionless and wrapped in a silence so profound it seemed as if time had stopped.

And then Sophy turned and saw Ben. Her face lit up in a smile and, like a spell being broken, William held up his arm in an ancient gesture, the clock chimed, and the cat jumped on to the window-sill, lashing its tail and showing small white teeth as it mewed to come in from the rain.

An hour later, fed, and, much to his surprise, washed again, Sophy presented Ben to William at his bench. William wore a green apron, his sleeves were rolled up and his red hair was tousled. Like that he did not seem a fearful figure but a workman, at home with tools, a bread-and-butter man.

On the bench was a picture. Sophy placed her hands on Ben's shoulder and urged him forward.

'Take a look, Ben,' she said. ' 'Tis a print William has made.'

Ben snatched at the print. A boy, black and wretched, with a huge burden on his back, crept through streets thick with snow. At the end of the street people were assembled in a small room.

William leaned forward almost anxiously. 'Do you like that?' he asked.

Ben pulled a face. 'No,' he said. 'I like pictures with soldiers on them, all shooting, and I like them that show highwaymen being hung. Them's the ones I like.'

William's face fell and Ben, impressed that his words should have such an effect on a grown man, adopted a reckless, swaggering air.

'I saw a picture once of a man having his head chopped off. It was coloured, that was, and all the blood was spurting in the air.'

Behind him he heard Sophy sigh. 'Don't you like those pictures?' he asked.

'Indeed I don't,' Sophy said firmly. 'Such cruelty is shameful. But see this print, 'tis a boy like yourself, but look at what the world has done to him. They have blackened his body by making him sweep chimneys, and they would blacken his soul too, while they cant their hymns in church. Are you not sorry for him?'

'Me?' Ben was indignant. 'If I saw him I'd bash him for being all black!'

Sophy was shocked. 'Why, you were as black as he when we found you yesterday, but did William strike you for being dirty? No. Indeed your state was like a blow at his heart. It hurt him to see you so neglected, and it hurts him to hear you speak so.' She gave him a gentle push. 'Now, try to be sorry for such words.'

Ben heard the door click and realized, rather alarmed, that he was alone with William. The room seemed very quiet. A wasp droned in the window and from the street came a long dying cry: 'Wa-ater-cress, sweet and pure; wa-ater-cress, pure and sweet.' Ben met William's eyes.

'Maybe I wouldn't have bashed him,' he whispered. 'Not unless he bashed me first.'

10

There was a long silence. William's eyes did not flicker as he looked down at Ben. And then he laughed.

'I know,' he said. 'I have had my scraps, too. I fought a boy once in Westminster Abbey. I was drawing the Confessor's tomb when he sneered at me. Aye, I was up among the angels but I came down to earth and gave him a drubbing.'

He pointed to the picture. 'Do you really not like it?'

Ben was tempted to say yes, but he looked at William's open face and shook his head. 'No.'

William lifted up the print. 'I drew it for children,' he said. 'But you don't like it?'

Again Ben shook his head. 'It's got no colour,' he said.

'No. We put that on afterwards.' William turned away, talking half to himself. 'The words explain it, of course, but. . .'

On the bench was a press with a huge roller. William swung the handle, the roller turned, and a print slid out. Ben was startled.

'How did that come out of there?' he asked.

'Have you never seen a press?' William asked. 'Look, there is a plate of copper set in the table here. Do you see the marks on it? That is the picture I have made. I rub ink into the marks, put the paper on it, like this.' He carefully fed a piece of paper into the press. 'Then I turn the handle and —' The rollers ran over the plate, William stripped off the paper, and there was a picture on it.

Ben was fascinated by the simplicity of the action. 'Let me try, Mister,' he said.

'Why yes.' William slipped a paper in the press and stood back.

Ben seized the handle but the press was heavy. He heaved and swung but the rollers did not move.

'I did the mangle last night,' he cried. 'I got it all the way round.'

Once more he wrestled with the press. 'I could do it if I was bigger,' he shouted, defeated but undaunted.

'That you could, that you could.' William took Ben's arm and was distressed by its thinness. 'Your time will come,' he said. He swung the handle and a print came out.

'Your missus can do that,' Ben said. 'She can mangle like anything. You ought to let her do it.'

William smiled. 'She does. She helps me with all my work, and she is good at it.'

11

'Why do you do it?' Ben asked.

'I earn my living by it. Some of it, anyway. You can learn this craft too, if you wish.'

Ben was thoughtful, not knowing whether he wanted to learn anything or not; but as he watched William about his patient, careful work in the quiet room, he began to think that whatever was involved in learning it was likely to be better by a mile than making candles.

At noon William stopped working and took Ben into the kitchen. Sophy had made pease-pudding, and Ben ate and ate until even William began to look thoughtful.

After they had eaten, William went into the garden. Sophy gathered up the dishes and began washing them.

'How have you got on with William?' she asked.

Ben leaned on the slop-stone. 'I don't know what he's talking about half the time,' he confided. 'He's not bad, though.'

'Not bad!' Sophy was indignant. 'No kinder man ever lived. What William says may be strange to you now, but he speaks of things more marvellous than any man on earth can know. You will understand as you grow, and you will learn to love him, as he loves you.'

Sophy dried the plates, Ben helping and breaking one, and then, as they finished, a black shape passed the window and threw a shadow across the room.

Sophy was startled. She leaned forward and peered through the window. 'Why,' she said, 'it's Mr. Godwin. What can he want?'

She dried her hands and left the room, Ben at her heels. William was at the end of the garden and stooping over him was a tall, dark figure. As Sophy approached he raised his hat.

'Mrs. Blake —' he gave a thin smile — 'I have been in town with Mary, and thought I would call on you. Mary asked me to give you her compliments.'

Sophy bobbed a curtsy. 'It is kind of her,' she said. 'Pray return mine.'

'Yes.' Godwin looked over Sophy's shoulder at Ben. Sophy put her arm protectively on the boy's shoulder.

'This is Ben,' she said. 'He is to live with us.'

'I see.' Godwin let his eyes rest briefly on Ben, then turned back to William.

'You have not called on us for some time. We think that a

12

loss. In these days it seems a pity that men who share the same views do not meet together.'

'I agree,' William said. 'Men who share the same views should meet. I have always thought that.'

'So we still have the same beliefs?' Godwin's voice was heavy, the words fell from his mouth like stones.

'About some things.'

'And others?' Godwin pushed his head forward. 'Do we now see the world differently?'

William smiled. 'I would say, rather, that we see different worlds.' He raised his hand in an unselfconscious gesture, as if he was touching something invisible, and fragile.

There was a stiff, slightly embarrassed pause. Godwin straightened himself. 'Still. . . we would like to see you some day. Our door is always open.'

'And ours, too,' William said.

They walked down the garden to the road.

'Do you still attend that church, the one with the strange beliefs?' Godwin asked.

'The Church of Swedenborg? Occasionally. Their beliefs are not strange enough for us these days.' William's face was expressionless but his voice was light, almost mocking.

At the gate they paused. Godwin clapped his hat on. 'I see that you still have the Lunatic Asylum as a neighbour,' he said.

'Yes, we have.' William sounded amused. 'But we think that there are people walking the streets crazier than those who are locked away in there.'

Godwin was impatient. 'Reason and logic tell us that —' he began, but William cut him off.

'Reason and logic do not tell us about the human soul. Read *King Lear* and tell me who is sane, Edmund or the Fool.'

'Humf.' Godwin blew out his cheeks. 'Well, we would be glad to see you.' He bowed at Sophy and strode off, black, angular, and determined.

William leaned on the gate, his face quizzical and good-humoured. 'Our social life is expanding,' he said. 'An invitation to tea!'

Sophy did not seem pleased by the announcement. Her face had lost its good humour and looked strained.

William put his arm around her shoulder. 'Come now,' he said. 'We must not let such chances slip. Think of it, an afternoon with Godwin! Two hours of having our brains examined! Don't tell me that doesn't tempt you.' He looked into Sophy's eyes. 'You are not afraid of meeting Mary, are you? I promise you, that is over, no need to fear.'

'No,' Sophy whispered. 'I will not be afraid.'

'That's my Sophy,' William said. 'What have we to fear from anything?'

They leaned on the gate for a while, quiet in the sunny afternoon. Then Ben cocked his head, as alert as a dog. In the distance was the rattling of a drum.

'Soldiers,' Ben said.

'Aye, soldiers.' William's voice was grim. 'Listen!'

The drum rattled and tapped away beyond the houses, the breeze bringing its sound to them, and carrying it away.

'Was there ever such a vile sound?' William said. 'It has neither tune nor harmony. Listen, it is like the beating of a machine. Godwin talked about the Asylum; harmless innocents are locked away in there while the Government put guns and bayonets in the hands of ruffians.'

He stalked off into the garden. The drum taps died away into the distance.

'Where are the soldiers going?' Ben asked.

'To France,' Sophy said. 'To stop the Revolution.'

'Are you afraid of the soldiers?'

Sophy smiled. 'No.'

'Why are you afraid of that man, the one who was here?'

'Mr. Godwin? I am not afraid of him,' Sophy said. 'He and William were friends once, but now. . . times change, people change.'

Ben nodded, as though theories of friendship were old knowledge to him. 'But who is Mary?' he asked. 'William said that you were afraid of her.'

Sophy's face tightened a little. ''Tis nothing for you to think of, Ben.'

She turned and walked up the path but half-way she stopped. 'I will say this lest you fret yourself. William did some work for her once. She and I fell out. I thought — well, I thought that she and William were too friendly. Now William thinks that I fear her. . . her sharp tongue. That is all.'

Ben swung on the gate, listening for the sound of the drum. He rather liked soldiers. He wondered why William had been so sharp about them. Everyone knew, even he, Ben

Pendrill, that the soldiers were fighting the French, and that the French had done something terrible — although he was less clear about what that was. A little rain began to fall. Ben held back his head, trying to catch the drops on his tongue. He thought that he might tell Sophy that if he could find Mary he would bash her, then Sophy wouldn't be afraid. The rain fell a little heavier and he backed to the house, still with his mouth open, as though he was sticking out his tongue at the heavens, and whatever they might contain.

Chapter 4

No one at the Blakes' asked Ben to work. He was free to do anything, or nothing, as if he was on holiday, or in an extended convalescence from some strange unnamed disease, which, in a sense, he was. For a few days he dawdled about the house, swinging on the garden-gate, or getting in Sophy's way as she went about her work. He sometimes went into the work-room and watched William at the press, although he did little more than look, and William never spoke unless he was spoken to.

At first Ben thought that he could carry on like that for ever, vacant, mindless, but he felt growing in him a desire to do something, to use his hands, to stretch his mind a little, to make something.

He began to haunt the work-room, silently watching as William silently worked. One day he went in and found William engraving a plate, finishing the picture he had started the day he first saw Ben.

Even Ben could see that the work called for minute and undivided attention as William bent over the gleaming plate, cutting line after delicate line. Ben edged nearer and nearer until he was breathing down William's ear. Then William looked up.

'Do you know what I am doing?' he asked.

Ben moved back cautiously, shaking his head.

'It is how pictures are made ready to be printed,' William said.

He picked a print from a jumble of papers. 'Look.'

Ben frowned over the print. It was a picture of a street, crowded, tumultuous. Ben knew that street. He had wandered through a hundred like it in his brief life. He knew the drunkards who lurched along it, and the blowsy women who lolled by its tavern door, and the deformed beggars who squatted in its filth, and the children with bent limbs who hobbled in its gutters. He knew the whole of its misery, and its degradation, and its savage energy.

'It's a good picture,' he said. 'Did you do it?'

'No.' William shook his head. 'It is by an engraver called Hogarth. But see the way it is done. The picture is made of lines. In the shadows the lines are thick and close together. But where there is light the lines are spaced apart, and thin. Do you see that?'

Ben did, and William nodded in satisfaction. 'Good; all engraving is done like that, cutting lines in metal. It is what I am doing now with this.' He waved his hand contemptuously at the girl with her roses and the dog. 'It is called intaglio work; that is an Italian word and it means to cut. That is what engravers do, cut. Would you like to learn how to do that? To cut?'

Ben looked at the copper plate, with its intricate pattern of lines. His gaze wandered to the print by Hogarth. He rather thought he would like to be able to cut pictures like that.

'Yes,' he said.

William was pleased. He took a piece of wood and a tool, a slender lance of steel with a triangular point.

'We must start you on wood,' he said. 'Copper is too expensive.' He held up the tool. 'This is a graver. Watch.'

He held the graver delicately but firmly, placed it on the wood, and cut a perfectly straight line, six inches long.

'That is the engraver's art,' he said.

'Is that all?' Ben said, with a note of scorn in his voice.

William's lips moved into the faintest of smiles. 'That is all. Try it.'

Ben took the graver and, with perfect confidence, jabbed forcibly at the wood. The graver gouged in for a quarter of an inch, and stopped dead. He jabbed again and the graver broke.

William held out his hand and Ben darted back, his arm raised defensively. As if he had not seen the reflex, William took another graver and held it against the wood.

'Let the tool do the work,' he said calmly. 'Keep it at the same angle.' He scored a line, and another. 'There are no mistakes where the spirit is pure.' His strong, supple fingers moved again. 'And there are no punishments here, Ben, none at all.'

He took an inked roller and ran it over the wood. Then he placed a strip of paper over the wood and pressed it down. When he took the paper away there was an animal on it.

Ben whistled in surprise. 'It's a dog,' he said.

William was slightly offended. 'It's a lamb,' he said. 'Do you not know what a lamb is?'

'No.' Ben didn't.

'Well, that is one,' William said firmly, but he stole another glance at the sketch as he put it down.

All morning Ben cut lines in the wood. None of them was straight, none the same length, but he broke no more gravers and by noon, his tongue sticking out from between his lips, he had begun to sense the material beneath the graver's blade. It was the first skill he had ever known.

He was looking forward to the afternoon's work but, after dinner, William rose. 'I am going to the Church of the Swedenborgians,' he announced. 'I have heard that there is a man who goes there who sees visions.'

He went to put his coat on. When he had left the room Sophy looked thoughtfully at Ben.

'Why not go with William?' she asked.

Ben's face fell, but Sophy shook her head. ' 'Tis no use looking like that, as if the goblins were after you. You must go out sometimes and I cannot have you at my apron-strings day and night. Is it that you are afraid of William that you don't want to go?'

Ben hesitated over his answer. Although he was still wary of William some of his fear had ebbed away. But not to be afraid of William in the house was one thing; not to be afraid of him outside, in a strange-sounding church, was quite another.

'I don't know,' he answered truthfully. 'What's this church?'

Sophy smiled. 'It is not one such as the Church of England. It is a new church. A man called Swedenborg started it. William and I used to go there often, but now that we are growing up we look for deeper truths than we can find there.'

'Aren't you grown up now?' Ben asked.

'Get along with you.' Sophy ruffled Ben's hair. 'You can go with William. The air will do you good and you will meet people such as you have never met before.' She opened the window and sniffed the air. 'It is cold out. You need a good coat. There is one upstairs which belonged to William's brother.'

The coat turned out to be green and too big, but Sophy

18

turned back the sleeves and pinned up the tails.

'There now, you look as nice as can be. Doesn't he?' She appealed to William who had appeared at the door.

'Yes.' William who, in a blue coat and white stock, looked like a sturdy farmer, was impatient.

'Well, off you go,' said Sophy and they left the house, William striding out and Ben, his coat-tails flapping by his ankles, trotting behind him. Ben was thinking of the people they were going to see at the Swedenborg Church.

'Do they see ghosts?' he asked.

William paused in mid-stride. 'They are ghosts,' he said.

Chapter 5

Ben followed William for a quarter of a mile, but walked slower and slower, until, when they reached Westminster Bridge, he stopped. William was across the bridge before he realized that Ben was no longer at his heels. He turned and saw the boy staring at the wall of an oil-lamp shop.

He paced back across the bridge. 'Ben,' he said. 'Why are you standing here?'

Ben kicked at the wall and muttered something inaudible.

'What?' William placed his hand on Ben's shoulder.

'The ghosts!' Ben shouted.

William caught the last word. 'Ghosts?' he repeated. He peered eagerly at the wall. 'Do you see a ghost?'

Ben kicked the wall furiously. 'No!' he shouted. 'I'm not going to see them. I'm not.' He gave a tremendous sniffle. 'I'm not going.'

William was bewildered. 'What are you crying for? What is this talk of ghosts?'

'You said we were going to see them,' Ben accused. 'Just now.'

'Ah!' William's face cleared. 'I understand. But I don't mean ghosts as you think. I was not talking about sheets flying in graveyards, nor skeletons walking about. It is a way I have of talking of people. . . some people. . . those I believe dead to the real life.' He paused and sighed. 'It is difficult to explain. Many men do not understand me. Come here.'

He wheedled Ben from the wall, led him to the bridge, and heaved him up so that he could lean over the parapet. Below them the Thames sucked at its frayed and rat-gnawed banks, lined with warehouses as sombre as tombstones.

'Look up,' William urged.

Above the warehouses smoke from a hundred thousand chimneys drifted across a tawny sky. And above the smoke, white, majestic, floated the dome of St. Paul's.

'Do you see that dome?' William asked. 'It is an eternal arc. The Greeks in ancient times first drew it. It is a church,

20

and yet what does that dome represent? The glory of God? The love and pity of Jesus Christ? The pomp and vanity of worldly men? Virtue or hypocrisy? I have seen all those things in it in my time. And yet there are men on this river who have never seen it. Never seen it as they should see it. For them it is only a pile of stones. They cannot see with their imagination, only with their eyes, bound by the flesh as tightly as a convict by his chains.'

He leaned on the parapet, his eyes brooding and remote. 'One Easter I saw the pauper children going in there for the Holy Thursday service. I followed them in and sat with them under the dome with their guardians, and saw the whole of creation. I wrote a song about that. Nothing could have been clearer and yet there are men who say they cannot understand it. They mean they do not wish to understand for the truth would destroy them. What I am saying, Ben, is that you will not see things as they truly are unless you wish to. If you do not want to see ghosts or visions, then you will not — and you will have lost your reason for existing.'

He looked at Ben who was spitting at a boat going under the bridge.

'Do you understand?'

Ben watched his spit fall and miss the boat, then he slid down. He had not understood a tenth of what William had said but he had heard that there would be no ghosts.

'None?' he asked.

'None that you will see,' William answered.

There was something about William it was hard to deny, a quality one might fear but not mistrust. It was, and even Ben could see it, an honesty beyond all doubt. Without another word he turned and walked across the bridge. William walked with him, now carefully measuring his stride to the boy's. As they passed over the river the man who owned the oil-lamp shop crept from his doorway.

'You're mad,' he screamed. 'You're crazy! You ought to be in Bedlam, both of you.'

William turned and looked back at the black, capering figure. 'There is a symbol of our time,' he said evenly. 'I have it in mind to write a poem of these streets, and this river.'

He turned abruptly and walked on. Ben was disappointed that William had not returned and beaten the man, but he forgot his regrets as they strode through the streets of London, tumultuous with life, and seething with sorrow and pain.

The ancient face of the city through which William and Ben walked was changing. Whole streets were blocked off as houses which had looked on the faces of ancient kings shuddered and collapsed before an army of wreckers. As their walls collapsed, huge clouds of dust arose, darkening the skies, and the faces of those who walked beneath the sky.

Ben was excited by the savage energy. 'Why are they knocking everything down?' he asked.

William was contemptuous. 'Those who are destroying this city say that it is progress, but they lie in their teeth. They hate what is old for it puts to shame what is new. And what is new they put there because it pays more. The speculators claim to see a new world, but they have golden guineas instead of eyes, and where we see the stars, they see coins.'

As they went on, to the East End, they left the destruction behind them and came to streets narrower, more hemmed in, shabbier, quieter, until they turned into a dark and silent alley. At the end of the alley was a shop, and in the shop window was a wig on a dusty wooden head. The head was white and had a face crudely painted on it. Its eyes were black sockets, and as William and Ben entered the shop the eyes seemed to follow Ben, as if wondering what brought such a boy into such an alley, and such a shop.

Although a little bell jangled as they went in, William did not wait but strode through the shop into a long narrow room with a pointed roof. On one wall was a picture of an old man, dressed in black, with a little sword on his lap. Beneath the picture twenty or thirty people were sitting on benches. They were looking at the man in the picture but he was not looking at them. He was staring over their heads into eternity.

William and Ben stood in the doorway and a thin, pallid man tiptoed to them.

'Mr. Blake,' he whispered. 'We have not had the — er — pleasure of your company for some time, some time.'

'Mr. Crane.' William nodded in greeting. 'I hear you have a man here who sees beyond this world.'

Crane smiled nervously. 'Yes, yes, we have a new — er — prophet.'

Disturbed by the whispers, the people in the room began to move a little. There were muted coughs, chairs creaked, clothes rustled. Crane moved from one foot to the other, torn between the people and William. William solved his

22

dilemma for him by striding to a vacant bench, towing Ben in his wake.

Ben perched in the midst of the people. His bench was too high for him and he swung his legs, kicking the bench legs. Someone hissed and he shrank into his coat, peering from his collar like a small animal from its lair.

He peered furtively around at the people. Many of them seemed ordinary; middle-aged men and women; quiet, decent, in sombre clothes, with kind faces and mad eyes. Among them was a sprinkling of young men in workmen's clothes. In thin white faces their eyes were wide, ardent, as if seeing a shimmering vision of the New Jerusalem in the dingy room.

And here and there were other, queerer people. Some of these were too fat, others too thin. One who had an elongated and spotted neck, had hands which never stopped moving, touching his nose and ear, ear and nose, in an endless, self-contained ritual. They might have been freaks, but they did not seem so to Ben. In the dark world from which he came, a world which warped and twisted those not already twisted or warped, they would have seemed, all of them, entirely normal. Among them Ben felt quite at home.

Crane stole forward and raised his hands. 'Brothers and sisters,' he said, 'we have with us the painter, Mr. Blake. And he has brought with him a young – er – disciple.'

The people turned and stared at Ben. They seemed ready to stare at him forever, but Crane coughed for their attention.

'We have with us, as well, our new friend. One who has learned to follow our great leader, Count Swedenborg.' He swung his arm dramatically at the portrait. 'Yes, our teacher, he who spoke with the angels of Sweden and brought to us the news that the Day of Judgement has already taken place! Yes! in 1757! In that year, just thirty-nine years ago, the Spirits of the Just were freed from their rags of mortality and were born again to Eternal Life. We were born to Eternal Life!'

There was a sigh of approval from the little crowd. Crane licked his lips. 'And daily we make new friends. Men come with humility, the humility of the heart. Mr. Grale!'

In obedience to this call a man rose. He was fat and soggy, with a large white face on which hairy eyebrows twitched like caterpillars on a rotten turnip. He writhed a little, as if from shyness, or embarrassment, although it seemed to Ben that he was neither shy nor embarrassed.

The man smiled. It was not a pleasant smile. Two muscles on either side of his face bunched and pulled his lips taut.

'Friends,' he cried. 'Dear friends, I am new to you but I feel that we are old friends just the same. Count Swedenborg, that great man, has led us to new ways of understanding of many mysteries, deep mysteries, deep.'

There was a rustle of approval and Grale smiled his strange, mechanical smile.

'Very deep mysteries. Who would have thought that the world had all changed in 1757? Everything looks the same, everything feels the same, but it has all changed all right — me, you, London, the King, ... even the little rats and mice that run about — ' he paused, as if conscious that this sounded implausible — 'even that dear little boy there.'

He pointed at Ben who scowled back ferociously. Although there were many things Ben did not know, he had a philosopher's wisdom when it came to men with empty eyes smiling at him.

'Yes,' Grale continued, undaunted. 'And we know we have changed. We know the secret, not like the others.'

There was another deep murmur of approval. Grale had touched a profound need in his audience's souls. They knew the secret, they alone had seen it. What pleasure that gave them, the dull tradesmen, the ardent workmen, the youths and the freaks. They loved Grale then, and he loved them.

'We have learned to see visions,' he cried. 'Lovely visions they are, Holy Spirits and all like that, and little children playing with flowers.'

The people sighed with pleasure and an old woman whispered, 'Praise the great Count.'

'Yes,' Grale cried. 'Praise him, praise him!' He threw up his wet hands. 'Praise him indeed. And praise the visions we have from the other world. 'Friends.' He leaned forward and lowered his voice. 'Friends, I am one of those who have been blessed with visions! Yes, I had one last night! Listen, listen, and I will tell you about it, and if you have any, tell me what you have. I am writing a book and in this book I will tell all our visions. Last night I saw a ghostly spirit with a torch. It was setting fire to old buildings! There were Lords and tyrants in that old building, and soldiers, all in the building!'

The people moved restlessly, disturbed by the images of

destruction and fire. Grale spoke urgently.

'Has anyone here had a vision like that? Has anyone heard voices talking about burning or fighting? It seems to me that in these times, when the French have got rid of their wicked king, that the spirits might be trying to tell us about what we should do here. Think, if the world has all changed like the Count said, perhaps we should be ready to help it change more. So, if you have any thoughts or visions, tell me, so I can put it in my book.'

He paused invitingly, and William stood up. 'Mr. Grale,' he asked, 'where do your visions come from?'

Grale hesitated, his eyes flickered and his tongue slid between his lips like a worm. 'Why, from the spirit world.'

'Yes, where else?' William agreed. 'But do they come from Heaven, or from Hell?'

Grale grinned, baring yellow, shattered teeth. 'The good ones come from Heaven, and the bad ones from Hell.'

'And what do you mean by Heaven and Hell?' William persisted.

'What indeed? What indeed?' Grale turned to his audience and waved his hands. The audience muttered disapprovingly at William. Who was he? the mutter suggested. Who was he to come and challenge their prophet?

Grale seized the moment. 'These are deep matters, Mr. Blake. I would be glad to talk of them to you. I will talk of them. I would do it now, but — ' He shrugged, implying in the gesture that public opinion was against him. 'But I will call on you — allow me to call on you.'

In his turn William paused. The writhing figure of Grale was unattractive and yet. . . who was he to judge a man on his appearance? He made up his mind and gave a stiff bow. 'Very well, call on me if you wish. I live in Lambeth, 13 Hercules Building.'

'Yes.' Grale said. 'On the Surrey side. I will call on you, Mr. Blake, indeed I will.'

William bowed again and left the room with Ben. Crane hurried after them, urging them to stay, but William shook his head.

'This society has nothing for me, now, Mr. Crane. Once I thought that Count Swedenborg saw the truth, now I understand that he saw only a part of it.'

'But,' Crane began.

William raised his hand, and the silent gesture cut off

Crane's words. 'It is for every man to find the truth for himself. Maybe they will be different truths. I must leave it to you to find your truth your way. Good day.'

William and Ben left the shop, leaving Crane and Grale surrounded by their disciples. One of them, a young man with a high, uncontrolled laugh, followed them for a while, gibbering and shouting, before William drove him off. Then, in silence, William and Ben walked home through the blue twilight of the evening.

Chapter 6

As William and Ben made their way home, Grale, too, left the Swedenborgians. He walked north, away from the river, past St. Paul's, and through the warren of streets behind the Old Bailey. At the end of one street he ducked through a yard and into a hallway.

A line of men were lounging there. Grale elbowed through them to a scarred door and gave a furtive, supplicant's knock. There was no answer and he knocked again. The door opened a crack, an eye peered through, then the door closed again.

Grale turned away and joined the other loungers. None of the men looked at one another but, if their eyes did meet, a look of knowing contempt was on their faces as if to say, you are the same as I am, and I am the same as you — worthless.

At intervals the door at the end of the corridor opened a little, a finger beckoned, and a man went through. None of them returned the same way. Grale waited, and waited. Somewhere a great clock clashed the hours, and the quarters, a mist seeped into the hallway, under the door a yellow light glowed, and still Grale waited, grinning at the wall. And then the finger beckoned him.

He went into a poky room, dark enough to be a cellar. A lamp flickered and the air was smelly with its vapour. In a corner, behind a stack of ledgers on a battered desk, a man was sitting. He was a small man with ginger whiskers and a sour mouth who looked as if he had seen everything this world had to see and found all of it unpleasant, including Grale, who now stood before him like a dog waiting to be whipped.

Grale bowed. 'Mr. Ferril, Sir. Good evening, Sir. Grale, Hector Grale.'

Ferril opened a ledger and flicked through it. 'Smithfield? Levant Court?'

Grale nodded eagerly, as if Ferril had demonstrated an astonishing feat of the intellect. 'Yes, Sir, that's where I live, absolutely right, Sir.'

Ferril slammed his ledger shut. 'Well, what have you got?'

'Sir.' Grale's mouth began to twitch into a grin but he pulled his lips back. 'Sir, I have been watching some people in the East End. I have got friendly with them. Very queer people they are.'

He stopped, for Ferril was laughing. At any rate the sounds an animal might make if it was taught to laugh were coming from his mouth.

'Queer? They are all queer down there. What do you want to come telling me that for?'

'No, Sir.' Grale writhed. 'That would be no good, no good at all. But they aren't just queer. One of them talks against the Church of England. Crane he's called. He's a wig-maker and he says that all religion is wrong except his. And one of them speaks on Spa Fields where the agitators go. He is a chair-leg maker and went about with all the other chair makers last year, when they wore red hats when the Frenchies had their Revolution. And there is another one. He said it was good that the French killed their king. He sells sheep's heads in Islington, Sir.'

'Sells sheep's heads?' Ferril laughed again.

Sweat trickled down Grale's face. 'This lot, Mr. Ferril, they're mixed up with foreigners, Swedes. And they have visions, all about burning old buildings. They told me that just now. I was with them just now.'

'Were you?' Ferril sucked his teeth. 'Have they got any swords, muskets?'

'No, Sir, but — '

'Any stuff for fire-raising, faggots, gunpowder?'

Grale shook his head.

'Have they got any plots for overthrowing the Government, killing the Prime Minister? Anything like that?' Ferril was not concealing his malice.

'No, Sir.'

'Out.' Ferril jerked his head in dismissal.

'Sir.' Despair thickened Grale's voice. 'Sir, I've got no — '

Ferril shook his head, knowing before Grale said it what he was going to say. 'You don't expect to get paid for rubbish like this, do you? A lot of loonies having visions — what's that? London is full of them. You get paid by results here. You tell me about dangerous men who want a revolution and I'll see you right. But nothing gets you nothing. This money belongs to the taxpayer,' he said virtuously. 'We're not here to waste it.'

Grale raised his hands in supplication. Ferril shook his head, but Grale had desperation behind him.

'I met another man there, in the East End. He looked dangerous. He's a painter.'

'A painter?' Ferril tensed like a spider whose web had been plucked. 'What's his name?'

'Blake, Sir. William Blake.' A little bubble of saliva formed at the corner of Grale's mouth.

Ferril opened a ledger. 'Barton, Billington, Black. . . Blake. Blake, William. Engraver. Golden Square, Soho. Associate of Thomas Paine, traitor; Godwin, the atheist; Johnson, publisher of radical tracts, etc.' He looked up accusingly. 'An engraver.'

'Sir,' Grale's hands were trembling, 'they said that he was a painter — and that address is wrong. He lives in Lambeth. Hercules Buildings.'

Ferril tapped the table. It seemed to Grale that he tapped it for a hundred years. At last the tapping stopped. 'All right,' Ferril said. 'Keep an eye on him. If he is an engraver he might be doing some printing, treasonable pamphlets and so on. Painters and writers, they are a danger to honest men. But don't go round for two or three weeks. There's no hurry. Don't seem too eager.'

He picked up a pen, opened a ledger and wrote next to Grale's name, 'No. 37, 16 October, 1796. One guinea'. He hesitated, then scratched out the 'one' and wrote 'half'. He slid a coin across the table. Grale took it and knew that for Ferril he had ceased to exist. And yet he bowed and bobbed his head as he backed through the door.

Grale's home in Levant Court was a room in a reeking tenement off Newgate Street. There was a truckle-bed in the room, and an old box. Nothing else. Grale took off his stock and his shoes, dragged his box to the window and sat down. He had bought a bag of steaming tripe and he munched it as he looked down on the highway. Below him, through the cliffs of the city, flowed the endless life of London. Labourers went past, clerks and carpenters, seamen, ostlers, thieves, linkmen, drabs, hawkers, tailors, servants, beggars, murderers, saints, poets and hangmen. Grale watched them all, hour after hour, remote, isolated, friendless. Once he had seen a man tie a stone around a dog's neck and throw it into the Fleet River to the cheers of a crowd. And as Grale sat at his window, hour after hour, he wondered, as he did every night, whether to do the same thing to himself, and whether a crowd would cheer if he did. He really thought, though, that if he did, no one would notice.

Chapter 7

A few days slid by. Ben began to put on weight and his skin lost its deadly white pallor. He carried on with his engraving, gouging scraps of wood and metal, and he began to learn how to colour the small prints William designed. That was precise work, leaning over the page with a full brush loaded with green or red or tawny umber, tinting in the borders. The figures William and Sophy painted, for they were beyond Ben's skill. The words he ignored. He could not read and it was incomprehensible to him that he ever could but, as the days passed, he found himself brooding over the letters, tracing them with his finger, and even mumbling sounds, although the sounds had nothing to do with the words before him.

But Sophy watched him and, one afternoon, she led him into the parlour and sat him next to her at the fireside. On her lap she had the cat and, in her hand, a small book, delicately coloured. On its cover was a woman with two children at her knee. A tree spread its boughs across the page and, among its branches, like leaves, words were intertwined.

Sophy ran her finger across the page. *'Songs of Innocence'* she read. 'You know, Ben, that William wrote these songs. He wrote them and printed them by a special way, which only we know. It is a secret, but we will teach you that secret, Ben.' She smiled. 'You know that when we have made these books we sell them?'

Ben nodded. He knew that.

'Yes,' Sophy said. 'We sell to those who will buy. Not that there are many of those. Look at this town, there are men in it who can't engrave no more than a blind man can, and painters who daub untruths, but the world beats a path to their doors and presses wealth upon them. Yet William has to go for work cap in hand — well, not begging, for he would never do that, but having to ask. To be sure if he would change and be like all the others he could have work, but he will never do that, never. We will live like free people!'

She struck the arm of the chair with such vigour that the cat jumped from her lap.

'There, there,' Sophy said. 'Now see what I've done, frightened poor puss. She picked up the cat and stroked its neck. 'When I talk of the printers who won't give William work, and the booksellers who won't stock his books, I always do get upset. But there, what do they matter? We will live by the truth. But I was going to start you reading, if you wish. Would you like that, Ben?'

Yes, Ben had decided that he would like that, he would like it very much.

'That's a good boy,' Sophy said approvingly. 'Now, here is a poem I like. You will learn your letters from it, and other things, too. You may not understand it all now but the meaning will grow in your heart, and you will be changed by it.'

She cleared her throat and began to read, moving her finger slowly from word to word:-

'To Mercy, Pity, Peace, and Love,
All pray in their distress;
And to these virtues of delight
Return their thankfulness. . .

For Mercy has a human heart,

33

Pity a human face,
And Love, the human form divine,
And Peace, the human dress.

Then every man, of every clime,
That prays in his distress,
Prays to the human form divine,
Love, Mercy, Pity, Peace.

And all must love the human form,
In heathen, Turk, or Jew;
Where Mercy, Love, and Pity dwell
There God is dwelling too.'

Sophy smiled at Ben. 'I do not think that you have had much of those things in your life, Ben, wherever you came from. They are not things the world desires today, when all men talk of is money. But this poem is a blow against wickedness and evil. People say that William is mad, but was there ever anything more sane than this song? But then you scarcely know what the words mean, do you?'

No, they were more of the multitudinous things of which Ben knew nothing. But something stirred within him as he felt his ignorance, something as improbable as roots from a seed — and Sophy saw it.

'Mercy, Ben,' she said. 'That is not to strike a blow when your enemy is at your mercy; and Pity, that is to feel for all in distress what the Good Samaritan felt for the fallen stranger; and Peace, that is to live together without wrath or fear. And Love. That is to feel for all what William and I feel for you.'

For an hour or so after that they went over the letters together. Later, Sophy sent Ben into the garden while she made the supper.

Ben wandered under the trees, chanting his alphabet: 'A. B. C. D. E. F. G. A. B. C. D. E. F.G.' He sauntered down to the gate and swung on it. 'Mercy,' he said. 'M.E.R.C.Y. Pity. P.I.T.Y.'

A dog padded past, limping on a wounded foot, its coat gleaming in the drizzle. 'Peace,' Ben said to it. 'P.E.A.C.E.' But the dog went on, its path as unswerving as an arrow.

Then came an apple girl, bare-headed in the rain, swinging her baskets easily over her strong shoulders.

'Love,' Ben said. 'L.O.V.E.'

The girl laughed and swung her hair. 'Impudence,' she cried, but she threw Ben an apple.

Ben caught the apple, as surprised as if it had fallen from Heaven. He rubbed it on his sleeve and bit into its sweet white flesh. A dizzying exhilaration filled his mind; from an animal blankness it had come full to bursting with words and images and ideas. He thought of William and Sophy, Godwin and Grale, and the Swedenborgians, and ghosts and visions, and engraving, and poetry, and St. Paul's, and the great river, and the colossal, grinding city beyond it. And there, on the quiet, rainy street, swinging on the gate, his growth from innocence began.

Chapter 8

The weather broke. Vast, unmoving clouds hung over the city. Endless raindrops fell heavily on the window-panes, blurring the outside world. Mists curtained the garden, making the house seem isolated, remote, as far from Lambeth as a Hebridean island lost in its fogs. A day passed, a week, another week; nobody called, no beggars came, no pedlars. The Asylum was hushed, there were no cries, no animal whoops. Sophy, William and Ben lived like castaways, self-sufficient, self-contained.

Ben cut away with his graver and presented his hacked and scarred pieces to William, like a heathen making an offering to an idol. But William was as indifferent as any block of stone and looked at Ben and his work through his pale eyes as though they were wraiths, as intangible as smoke.

William was haunted by the vision of a huge, untamed animal he had seen on the day he had met Ben. Now, words were drifting to the image, giving it shape and clarity. The image and the words were growing together as imperceptibly, but as surely, as crystals on a window in a frost. And although the image had been born in darkness it was growing in brightness, burning like a brand, or a star. Already the image had been named. Tiger, William thought. Tiger. And for days he hardly spoke, unless it was to what only he saw, and scarcely listened, unless to what only he heard.

But Ben cut on, line after line, each straighter, each longer, and in his concentration he became as self-contained as William. And he found William's talking to himself less strange, for now he constantly talked to himself. He did this the more for his mastery over words was growing. Every afternoon he sat with Sophy reading the *Songs of Innocence*. Strange songs he found them, too. They were pictures of childhood, although such a one as he had never known, and pictures of joy, but never simple joys. It was as if the children in the *Songs* were playing just beyond the range of a shadow which was always creeping out to them, and a shadow the

36

darker because it was never clear what was hidden in it, although something was.

'Why does William write these songs?' Ben asked.

'It is the lust to create,' Sophy answered. 'Who does not have it?'

'Not many men write songs,' Ben objected. 'Not many men make pictures.'

'No,' said Sophy. 'But they can sing or dance.'

'Not all men do those, either,' said Ben, thinking of Carlin, the candle-maker.

Sophy thought for a moment. 'That is true. But if a man does none of those things, then he is not truly a man.'

And, thinking again of Carlin, Ben agreed with that.

But Sophy did not read only from the *Songs*. There were many books in the house and Sophy might take one down at random and read it with Ben. Some of them Sophy herself could hardly read and these were put aside. But there were finds: Milton, whose huge incantations Ben relished if he did not fully understand:

'. . . profoundest hell,
Receive thy new possessor — one who brings
A mind not to be changed by place or time.
The mind is its own place, and in itself
Can make a heav'n of hell, a hell of heav'en.
What matter where, if I be still the same,
And what should I be, all but less than He —
Whom thunder has made greater? Here at least
We shall be free; the Almighty has not built
Here for His envy, will not drive us hence:
Here we may reign secure, and in my choice,
To reign is worth ambition, though in hell:
Better to reign in hell than serve in heav'n.'

There was a ferocious story of persecution and terror called *Caleb Williams*, which, much to Ben's surprise, was by the sombre Godwin. One day Sophy took down a green book. 'This is a famous book, Ben,' she said. 'It was written against tyranny and oppression, and it struck such a blow that the Government hounded the writer to France. They might have hanged him had he stayed here. It is called *The Rights of Man*. Do you see the author's name? It is Tom Paine.'

And then a cold wind blew from the East, blowing away
the rain and mist. When it stopped, the leaves had fallen from
the trees, and William had written another song.

He read it to Ben and Sophy in the evening, before the
fire. Sophy had her sewing and Ben sat with his legs
stretched, nonchalant, jaunty, self-confident in his new found
health and knowledge. But his cocky air faded as William
read his song:

> 'Tiger! Tiger! burning bright
> In the forests of the night,
> What immortal hand or eye
> Could frame thy fearful symmetry?
>
> In what distant deeps or skies
> Burnt the fire of thine eyes?
> On what wings dare he aspire?
> What the hand dare seize the fire?
>
> And what shoulder, and what art,
> Could twist the sinews of thy heart?
> And when thy heart began to beat,
> What dread hand? and what dread feet?
>
> What the hammer? What the chain?
> In what furnace was thy brain?
> What the anvil? What dread grasp
> Dare its deadly terrors clasp?
>
> When the stars threw down their spears,
> And water'd heaven with their tears,
> Did he smile his work to see?
> Did he who made the Lamb make thee?
>
> Tiger! Tiger! burning bright
> In the forests of the night,
> What immortal hand or eye,
> Dare frame thy fearful symmetry?'

The forests of the night, Ben wondered, what forests were
they? And what tigers haunted them? He felt afraid,
suddenly in danger, for it occurred to him that perhaps the
landscape of darkness was not a real one but something in

38

William's mind — perhaps it was William's mind; and follow-ing that thought, like a shadow, came another; maybe the tiger was not real either, but an idea in William's mind. He looked wonderingly across the fire at William and felt a surge of admiration for a man who would open his mind like that for anyone to look inside it. He would not like to open his own mind.

'I am thinking of making a new book,' William said. 'It will have many songs of this kind. Has Ben seen the *Songs of Innocence*?'

'Indeed he has,' Sophy said. 'He has been learning his letters from them, haven't you, Ben?'

'Yes.' Ben straightened, ready to show his prowess as a scholar there and then, but William had other interests.

'That is good. But has he understood the meaning? With-out that he has merely clamped fresh fetters on his mind. Many men can read, but how many men know what to read? There are men in this city who would think the lad insane if they saw him with anything but a bill of lading in his hand.'

'He knows the *Songs*,' Sophy said.

And that was true, Ben thought. He did know them now. Not merely to whisper as he bent over his graver, or repeat like a parrot in a cage, but as part of his inner life, like knowing his heart was beating.

'Yes, William,' he said. 'I know the *Songs*.'

'You do, Ben,' William said. 'I know by the way the fire catches on your face.' Although his voice was gentle his face was grim. 'But my new songs will not be of innocence. They will be of errors and evil and rebellion. It will be a dangerous book to write, and a more dangerous book to read, for if knowledge is dangerous, then what menace will eternal know-ledge bring?'

'What will you call this book, William?' Sophy asked.

'I shall call it *Songs of Experience*,' William said. 'Enough has been said of innocence. I shall speak to the world in a language it understands.' He leaned forward. 'You are a changed being, Ben. Truly I think that you have been born again. It may be that now you are remade you will work on my book with me. Do you wish that?'

'I am sure he will,' Sophy said. 'He has worked hard all the week, cutting away with never a word from you to keep him going.'

'Has he now?' William smiled, and it was like a curtain

being drawn from a window. 'Then he has worked well, for he has worked for the love of his craft. And he has done it in secret when he thought none saw. But God saw, God saw.'

The clock chimed the hour. Sophy lifted her head. 'I must shop tomorrow,' she said. Her voice was casual. William stirred restlessly in his chair. 'I know what that means.' He looked across at Ben. 'When people live together for a long time they learn to speak a secret language. What Sophy is saying is that she is short of money so I must go to the booksellers and try to sell my work.'

'I am sorry, William.' Sophy was contrite.

'I know, my dear. It is not for you to apologize, but rather me. I will go.'

'We will all go,' Sophy said. 'The air will do us good.'

'Aye?' William's voice was dry. 'I doubt not that they say the same thing to condemned men when they take them out to hang them. But we will go.'

William said no more and they sat in silence. The only sounds were the ticking of the clock and the purring of the cat. Ben had never known such stillness. It was as if William could summon up silence when he willed, like a magician.

Ben watched William now. He was looking into a dark corner of the room, not idly but intently. Ben felt impelled to look over his shoulder, but there was nothing there. Nothing that he could see, anyway. And when he turned back to the fire, William had gone.

Chapter 9

Ben was excited at the thought of going to the booksellers. He was up early — and had his first surprise. Sophy had bought him a suit of clothes and a pair of shoes from a second-hand clothes hawker. The suit was russet and in it Ben looked as light as an autumn leaf. When he looked in the mirror he scarcely recognized himself.

'Is that me?' he wondered. 'Is it really me?'

Assuring himself that the reflection was really and truly Ben Pendrill, he waited impatiently while William made a final selection of the work he was taking to the booksellers.

At last William had made his choice and the three of them, man, woman, and youth, crossed the bridge into the city. They did not talk. Sophy was wistful and William had a tight, stubborn face; but Ben was too lost in his own sensations to notice this.

Before, when he had walked the streets, Ben had been hardly aware of them; his eyes, then, sick holes in a white face. Like an animal he had seen only what mattered to his survival: an arm raised to strike a blow; a snarling dog, ready to bite; a scrap of food left unattended. Now, fed, clean, dapper in his russet suit, his shoes tapping lightly over the cobbles, he began to see a step beyond survival, seeing not merely through his eyes, but with the shaping power of his imagination. The threatening arm was raised in fear; the dog, mangy and starving, bared its teeth in anticipation of a blow; the food was another's grasp on life.

They walked along the Strand towards Fleet Street. Where Arundel Street ran down to the river, the way was blocked by a line of red-coated soldiers. Between the soldiers a file of men, chained together, hobbled down to the wharf. Misery and despair were on their faces and at the sight of their wretchedness even the London crowd was silent. The only sounds in the street were the shuffling of feet and the clanking of manacles.

'Where are those men going?' Ben asked.

Sophy pressed his hand, her face creased with anguish. 'They are convicts going to be transported, maybe to Van Diemen's Land. They will never see their own land again, poor souls.'

'What have they done?' Ben wanted to know, but this time it was William who answered, his voice ringing across the street like a trumpet call.

'They have sinned against Man, but those who have enslaved them like this sin against the Holy Ghost.'

The people next to the Blakes stirred uneasily and tried to edge away from them. A soldier in front of them turned his unshaven face and scowled. But then a mounted officer clattered past, shouting orders, and the soldiers and the convicts moved on.

The crowd broke up, and under the shadow of Wren's dome the Blakes and Ben walked up Fleet Street and turned into St. Paul's Churchyard.

Along one side of the square were a line of bookshops, their windows gaudy with prints. Ben was ready enough to dawdle there, but, with the air of a man going to his execution, William walked grimly into the first shop. Sophy, equally unhappy, took Ben's hand and followed.

There were several customers in the shop, stooping over books and pictures, assistants fluttering around them. Behind a counter, on an elevated chair like a throne, sat a man with a look of permanent, quiet enjoyment on his face. It is possible that when a customer bought a book his look of pleasure deepened, but beyond that he seemed immune from human stress. But then he saw William and his good humour vanished.

With an air of enormous reluctance he climbed down from his throne and approached the Blakes.

'Sir.' He inclined his head an inch towards William, and a further inch towards Sophy. Ben he did not see at all. There was scarcely concealed irritation in his voice as he asked William what he wanted, and scarcely hidden disdain in his eyes as he looked at William's work.

'Very interesting, Mr. Blake — as usual. I see that you are still set in your ways. Yes, yes. . .' Idly he flipped through the prints. 'Your work becomes more. . . individual than ever. This.' He pointed to a picture. Two beings, one clothed in light and the other in flames, confronted each other across a blue abyss. 'What is this? What can it mean?' He raised his eyes and looked about, as if seeking the answer on the ceiling.

William leaned forward, eagerly, seriously. 'They are two angels. One is from Heaven and the other from Hell. Each is cloaked in the spirit of its own world, but as yet neither can see the virtue of the other.'

'Virtue, Mr. Blake? Virtue? What virtue can there be in Hell?'

Again the bookseller cast his eyes about. This time an assistant appeared, summoned by the gaze. He, too, looked at the print and his lips pursed, as though repressing a titter.

William was unaware of this. He answered the question as though it was a serious request for information. 'I do not mean Heaven and Hell in the common sense. When I say Heaven, I mean the world of innocence, and that is good; by Hell, I mean knowledge born of experience; that is, true knowledge. These pictures are to teach the meaning of the universe in which we live.'

But the man was not listening. 'I have a bookshop and I sell books and prints. I do not own a school of allegory. Perhaps you should find a shop which sells allegories. I do not. I sell polite books, my customers are polite. What have they to do with Heaven and Hell? Besides which, Mr. Blake, your style of picture-making is old-fashioned.'

At his elbow the assistant nodded, then shook his head, agreeing with the judgement, and condemning the work.

William flushed. 'My engravings are honest — '

'I say nothing about your honesty, Mr. Blake. But does honesty sell prints or pictures or books?' The bookseller's voice quivered slightly. 'I have lost money on you, Mr. Blake. The *Songs of Innocence* —' He paused as if mastering the memory of some grievous injustice. 'Learn another style, Sir. Colour your work differently, learn to draw, learn to see the world as every other man does, then — ' he bent forward with the manner of one doing enormous and meritorious work — 'then, perhaps, we might discuss the matter again. In the meantime, we must give the public what it wants. Good day, Sir, Ma'am.'

An assistant appeared at William's elbow, and another at the door. William slammed his folio shut and looked up, ready to retort, but the bookseller was back on his throne, aloof, immune, waiting to give the public what he conceived it wanted.

Sophy and Ben trailing behind him, William walked along the street, and into another shop. Before William had time to open his folio the proprietor had waved them out. The next shop William entered alone. Within a minute he had reappeared, slamming the door behind him with such fury that the glass rattled, his face white with rage and humiliation.

Sophy took his arm. 'Don't let them upset you, William,' she said. 'What do they know about art? They might as well be selling fish.'

'Aye? I knew that before we set out this morning,' William said bitterly. 'And where now? Do I hawk my work on the street?'

Sophy twisted her hands but from some well of moral courage she raised a cheerful smile. 'We, we could go to Godwin's. There are often people at his house and someone might. . .'

'Might?' William was savage. 'Might buy a picture? Yes. And we might see Godwin flying over Hyde Park, miracles do happen.' He swung on his heel and strode off.

Sophy and Ben followed William. Ben was thoughtful. 'I thought that you didn't want to go to Godwin's,' he said.

'It will give William more pain than it gives me,' Sophy answered. 'We are a little too like charity children today.'

Their way to Godwin's led them from the narrow lanes of the City into the West End. For Ben it was a new experience. He was open-mouthed at the elegant streets and squares, where opulent carriages, polished like glass, waited outside gilded doors, and enormous footmen dawdled by the area railings. Across one square he saw the flash of steel and heard the blare of bugles.

'Can we go and watch?' he asked.

William heard him and turned round, fire in his eyes. 'You wish to see the soldiers? You wish to see muskets and bayonets? Go then, and then go to the shambles and see the butchers slaughtering sheep.'

Ben fell back before the outburst but Sophy took his arm. 'Now, William,' she said. 'It is only a boy's fancy.'

William said no more but strode away. Sophy led Ben on. 'There, Ben,' she said. 'Never fear. William did not mean what he said. He is upset. It is not a nice thing for a man to see his work sneered at by such as the booksellers, and a more bitter one to have to go to Godwin's hoping to sell work. But he will be sorry for what he said and love you again. Come, now, and don't be frightened. All will come right before the day is out.'

Somewhat subdued, Ben went along, watching William's blue clad back carefully, and thinking that the tiger in the man had shown its claws.

They crossed Oxford Street and soon entered a small cul-de-sac which had a quiet, unpretentious house at its end. In answer to William's knock a woman opened the door. She was not tall and was dressed in a severe brown dress, without ornament or decoration, and, although she was handsome, she had a determined manner, a stand and deliver air, like a bandit of the intellect.

'Well, Mr. Blake,' she said, 'we did not look for you today. We have started tea. Once we would never have done so without your presence, but the world does not wait forever. Is that not so, Ma'am?' She rounded on Sophy in a challenging way.

'No, Miss,' Sophy said, rather stressing the Miss. 'But we have been making calls and were delayed. Not that I am ever very sure of the time, myself.'

'But then, Ma'am, is that not being vague?' Miss Wollstonecraft said this in a piercing way, as though she were sticking pins into Sophy. 'Surely it is a great crime to be vague. Is that not to misuse our faculties?'

'Well, that may be so,' Sophy answered. 'But perhaps I am vague. We all have our faults, I suppose, and must learn to live with them.' She slipped her cloak off, her full figure making the other woman seem shrunken.

Miss Wollstonecraft opened her mouth to speak but was interrupted by Godwin's heavy voice.

'Mary, bring the guests in. Show the mettle of your mind here.'

Miss Wollstonecraft seemed disinclined to heed the command but Sophy brushed past her into the room. Ben slid around Mary and peered through the door. In a green parlour a group of people were gathered by a table which had on it a silver teapot and elegant china cups.

Godwin stepped forward. 'Mrs. Blake, your servant, Madam. And William? Is he there?' His eyes fell on Ben. 'And I see you have your new lad,' he added, without enthusiasm.

He turned to William. 'I think you know most of the company. Mr. Parker, Mr. Stothard; Mr. Butts I think that you have not met before.' Butts, a pleasant-looking man in his fifties, smiled genially. William shook hands with Butts, although without any sign of pleasure, and retired into a corner. Mary Wollstonecraft's penetrating voice drilled across the room.

'How interesting to have found the child, Mrs. Blake. Tell us, do you find his mind a true *tabula rasa*?'

Sophy shook her head. 'That I can't say, Miss, for I don't know what it is.'

'Why,' Mary cried, 'it is from the Latin, Ma'am, and means a blank sheet. The mind, if a *tabula rasa*, is as empty of sensation or knowledge as a clean sheet of paper is of writing. The image is Mr. Locke's the philosopher. It is a question of great importance; are we born with knowledge, or do we acquire it?'

'If what Mr. Locke says should be true then I am afraid that Ben's mind will have many a foul thing scrawled on it. But I don't like to talk so of the child. Let him be.'

Mary leaned forward. 'Come now, we cannot let anyone just be. The world will not let anyone be. The child is a splendid subject for an experiment in education on truly rational lines. You must ask Mr. Godwin for his advice. He has the most original views on education. Will you not accept his help?'

'I am always glad of anyone's help,' Sophy said. 'Perhaps Mr. Godwin will help me with the washing?'

Godwin lifted his saturnine face. 'I hardly think that, Mrs. Blake. It would not be rational for me to do so. My talents do not lie in the direction of washing, although yours may.'

A little genteel burst of laughter greeted this sally, not all of it good-humoured. Sophy flushed and looked across at William, who was scowling at his shoes. But Mary had not finished, and it seemed as if William's silence encouraged her to press Sophy further.

'Surely you agree with Mr. Godwin,' she demanded. 'Would it not be irrational for him to waste his gifts washing and cooking?'

'If you say so, Ma'am.' Sophy was curt. 'I do not pretend to be clever.'

Mary was remorseless. 'It is not a question of being clever. Surely you know that I have long argued that washing, and cooking, and the caring for children, should not be the sole burden of women. Why should not some men do them, and why should not women do the things men do? Why should

46

not women be educated?'

'I know that you have said these things,' Sophy said. 'And indeed I am not clever but I have learned to read and write.'

'And commendably.' It was Butts who spoke in a clear voice. 'I am sure we are all agreed on that.'

There was a murmur of agreement, although not from all the people in the room.

Stothard coughed. 'I see that you have a folio with you, Mr. Blake. Have you any new pictures you might care to show us?'

William stirred in his corner. 'Some are new, but what of that? What has newness to do with art? The painters of olden times knew more of art than any since.'

'Why!' Stothard appealed. 'Surely, Mr. Blake, we live in new times. Great events are taking place among us. The French Revolution, surely that is a mighty new event. To throw down a king, Sir, a king and a wasteful, luxurious court, that is a great matter. And in England, are there not new machines, and new men running them? Indeed there are and they will alter our age. Come, Sir, you will agree with that?'

'I have heard of the French Revolution,' William said. 'When it took place I wore a red bonnet in the streets when some I knew gave it their plaudits over the tea-table. But you speak of the new age; I tell you this, Sir, these changes, and any others in the world, are without meaning unless men are changed in their hearts and learn to live in eternity.'

Parker was indignant. 'Live in eternity? Come, Mr. Blake. This is close to priest-craft.'

'Those words do not frighten me,' William said. 'We hear too much of priest-craft in these days. Let us hear a little more of soldier-craft, or business-craft, or politician-craft. I tell you that all ages are the same, but that genius is above the age. Look at Signor Raphael if you wish my proof.'

He looked about him challengingly, and Godwin took him up. 'This is to talk of what cannot be proven, or demonstrated. You are not talking of the world as it is but of your own feelings about it.'

'What of that,' William cried. 'Do you think that all there is in this world is what you see of it? Would you reduce us all to mathematicians, proving all we believe by logic? I tell you that there are things unseen of more truth than any eye has seen.'

Godwin shrugged. 'These are your fancies, William. If you choose to live in them. . . well.' He spread his hands over the teacups. 'I choose to deal with the explicable and the demonstrable. With the real world.'

There was an awkward silence, broken again by Butts. In his pleasant voice he asked William to show his paintings. 'As a favour, Sir.'

William looked at him. Butts' face was frank and open. Not, perhaps, a clever face, but an understanding one. Butts smiled.

'I confess I know nothing of logic, Sir.'

William opened his folio and spread out his work. Godwin stared at it expressionlessly. Parker leaned over his shoulder shaking his head and Butts faded away to the window and stared thoughtfully into the street.

Stothard sighed. 'There is not another man in London with your vision, Mr. Blake. But can you not help us to understand what you mean?'

'I heard the same thing not an hour ago,' William said. 'In a shop.' He gathered up the pictures and began shuffling them into his folio.

Stothard was conciliatory. 'I do admire your work, Mr. Blake.' He said. 'The *Songs of Innocence* — I never spent my money better.'

'I will remember that when I am eating my dinner,' William said. He made for the door.

Mary leaped before him. 'Promise that you will come again,' she cried. 'We have missed you, William, indeed we have.' She appealed to the company, who agreed, with varying degrees of enthusiasm. Butts made a point of thanking William for showing his paintings. In return, William was cold. 'Next time, perhaps, you will look at them,' he said.

Chapter 10

They left Godwin's and made their way home. The streets were choked with people but William walked through them heedlessly, banging into people and elbowing them aside. The sky was dark, almost purple, and the light made the faces of the people seem bruised, wrathful. Ben was uneasy, sensing in the jostling crowds and crashing noises of the city a simmering violence, needing little to spark it off.

But at Sackville Street they came upon a street market and were suddenly surrounded by the trilling of birds. On either side, in cages piled ten feet high, fluttering and twittering, were thousands of birds. Linnets, robins, larks and blackbirds, finches, warblers, tits, wagtails, siskins, ravens, crows, jackdaws; whatever had wings had been caught and imprisoned. Ben was entranced at the sight but William, his face already taut with stress, grew savage. At one stall he stopped. Two men were stooping over a bench. On the bench they had a raven, and they were slitting its tongue.

'Why do you do that?' William asked, his voice thick with anger.

One of the men looked up. Across his forehead he had a ragged scar.

'What are we doing, Guv? We are nicking its tongue to help it talk. They can't talk unless you slit their tongues, ravens can't, but if you cut them they'll chatter away as good as your missus. Take one home for her. Here's a beauty.'

'You villain,' William said. 'Is this how you live, slashing and maiming?'

The man stared at William, astounded. The other man lurched from behind the stall.

'What's it to you?' he growled. 'Who are you to come here calling us villains?'

At the sound of angry voices a crowd had begun to gather and the man raised his voice, appealing to it.

'You want to mind your own business instead of interfering with honest working-men. Call me a villain — go on and see

50

what you get!'

He shoved his fist under William's nose. His hand still held the bird.

'You are a villain,' William said. 'You are a mindless villain with the feelings of a block of stone.'

'Why,' the man spat, 'for two pins I'd kick your head in. Did you hear that?' He turned to the crowd. 'He called me a stone!' he said pathetically.

The crowd muttered angrily, as if personally abused. Someone shouted, 'Bash him.'

William swung around, his eyes flashing, his sturdy frame planted solidly on the cobbles. 'Who will be first?' he shouted.

No one seemed anxious for that honour and one or two timid souls decided to view matters from the back of the crowd rather than the front. Their departure was the signal for a general retreat. And, indeed, there was a daunting blaze in William's eyes. The bird men returned to their stall. William, after glaring about him, began to walk away; as he did so, one of the men shouted a vile name, cut off the bird's head, and flung it after him.

The fragments struck William on the back, but he did not turn again and walked on, catcalls and oaths following him.

The three, William, Ben and Sophy, walked back to the river, and home. The sullen evening laid its weight upon them and their footsteps dragged, even Ben's. He was lost in thought. Something was tugging away at the back of his mind. It was not until they reached the bridge that he realized what it was; the print by Hogarth which William had shown him had been like the scene in the bird-market; or was it the other way round?

On the bridge they paused and leaned on the parapet. William frowned down into the dusk.

'That man, the one in the bird-market, did you see his face?'

'Yes. It bore a scar. I see it on many a man's face, such a scar, such a mark. Cain bore one when he wandered the world after he had murdered his brother.'

In the dusk, under the arches of the bridge, the river, copper-coloured under the weary sky, flowed in its great curve to the sea. Downstream the buildings of the city stabbed into the sky while above them, like a distant mountain catching the last rays of the sun, shone St. Paul's.

William raised his hand. 'Godwin talked of reason today, but what reason do I find in this city? It is the sum of human misery. They are penning in the river.' He turned on his heel. 'Go home, Sophy.'

'Yes, William,' Sophy said. 'Shall I keep your dinner ready?'

'No. Care for yourselves.' William handed Sophy the folio and walked back across the bridge.

'Well,' Sophy said, 'it's one day I won't be sorry to see ended. Come along, Ben, 'tis only a step now.'

Together they walked down the quiet road, past the church, already tinged with soot, past the Lunatic Asylum, silent in its misery, and down to Hercules Buildings. As they reached their gate a figure stepped from the darkness. It was Hector Grale.

Chapter 11

Grale lifted his shabby hat and grinned into the darkness. 'Mrs. Blake? Do I speak to Mrs. Blake?'

Sophy stepped back, and Grale raised his hand. 'No need to be alarmed, Ma'am, I am a friend of your husband. Grale is the name, Hector Grale, at your service. This little chap here knows me, don't you, Tommy? Or is it Billy?'

Before Ben could dodge, Grale had clapped his hand on his head. The hand was clammy, and smelt of old bedclothes.

'I wonder if I could speak to your husband,' Grale went on. 'He invited me to come, didn't he, my boy?'

Ben's impulse was to deny ever having seen Grale, but he nodded reluctantly.

'Well.' Sophy was uncertain. 'Mr. Blake is in the city, walking, and what time he will be back I don't know.'

'I understand, walking in the city. I do a great deal of that myself,' Grale said. 'Walking in the city at night. Yes.' He grinned, apparently ready to stand in the road until Doomsday.

'Do you?' Sophy made to go up the path. Grale stepped after her.

'Mrs. Blake, Ma'am, I would be glad of a drink of water if I could impose on you. Just a drink of water, if it's no trouble.'

'Yes.' Sophy was contrite. 'Come along, Mr. Grale.' She led the way into the house. In the parlour Grale chose to sit in William's chair, much to Ben's disgust. If Grale noticed this he was unperturbed. He took the water and looked about him approvingly.

'A very nice house, Ma'am, a lovely house. And good water, clear and sweet. There is a great deal of bad water in London. It is very bad where I live. But this water is sweet on the tongue.'

He drank and sighed. 'I have been ill for some days, Ma'am, with a fever. I had sharp pains, just in my side, here, and a throbbing in my head.'

'I am sorry to hear it,' Sophy said with deep feeling. 'Who has been looking after you?'

'No one, Mrs. Blake. I live alone and there is no one to look after me if I am ill.'

His voice died away. The only sounds were the ticking of the clock and the cat purring before the fire.

Grale stirred. 'It is very noisy where I live. The carriages crash on the road, and the people in Levant Court are very wild and noisy. They stay up late, drinking gin, and shouting and quarrelling. It is not like this house.'

'Would you like some food, Mr. Grale?' Sophy asked. 'I have some broth which will nourish you.'

Grale was hungry and would have liked the broth but some obscure feeling of shame moved inside him. To his own surprise he found himself saying no.

'But I would like to look at Mr. Blake's pictures if I may. I like pictures, I have often thought that I would like to have one on my wall.'

'Of course.' Sophy was always ready to show William's work. She took Grale into the work-room and laid out some prints.

When Grale looked at them his eyebrows shot up and writhed on his forehead. 'What sort of pictures are these?' he asked. 'What is this?'

He pointed to a print of a man, naked, sitting on a rock, and leaning over a scroll with a pair of compasses in his hand.

'That is Newton,' Sophy said.

'Newton, Ma'am?' Grale was dumbfounded. 'Sir Isaac Newton, the man who discovered gravity?'

'Yes.' Sophy spoke earnestly. 'Do you see how William has drawn him? He is a man whose soul is caught in a trap of his making. He understands the world of matter and time, but only that. So William has drawn him there, brooding over his abstractions, while all about him lie the oceans of eternity which he cannot explore.'

Grale peered again at the picture in disbelief. 'Sir Isaac Newton,' he murmured. 'Newton! And what is this?' He held up a small picture. On a leaf was an insect's cocoon with a caterpillar blindly crawling by. The cocoon had the face of a human infant. Underneath the leaf were the words 'What is Man?'

'Ah,' said Sophy. 'The cocoon is the human soul, dreaming of immortality. Inside its wrapping it thinks that it can never change. But the caterpillar is man as he grows and is, blind and devouring, lost to the true treasures of the universe. Is it not beautiful?'

'It is amazing, Ma'am,' Grale said, sincerely. He was astonished by the pictures. In fact he was so surprised that he almost forgot why he was at the Blakes'. But then, as Sophy turned away to get some more of William's work, he saw a sheaf of paper. On it were the words, 'The French Revolution.'

Sophy showed Grale more prints, and a copy of *Songs of Innocence.*

'Wonderful,' Grale cried. 'Most remarkable. If I had any money I would buy a copy now. But what is that over there?'

As Sophy turned away to reach for the picture, Grale snatched up *The French Revolution* and stuffed it in his pocket. When Sophy turned to him again he was all attention, nodding, bowing, grinning. And he was still grinning when he made a hasty farewell a moment later and left the house.

Grale felt ill as he walked back to the city. Although the night was cold he was sweating, an ulcerous vein throbbed in his leg, and his dirty stock had rubbed a boil on his neck. Where he should have been was in bed; where he was going was the dark room behind the Old Bailey.

He had no doubt that Ferril would be there. In all the time that Grale had crept about London, furtively spying and informing, he had called on Ferril at all hours of the day and night. Only on Monday mornings had he ever found him absent.

And Ferril was there, crouched behind his books. As Grale stood humbly before the desk he wondered about the ledgers. How many people were in them, he thought, and by whose authority were they there? And who read Ferril's reports, and what happened to them then? Did Pitt ever see them? Or Liverpool? or Grenville? Or any of the other rulers of the land?

The thoughts passed through his mind as he watched Ferril scribbling away. Like that, with his head down, all Grale could see of him was a bald disc of head perched on a dirty green coat. As Ferril wrote, the bald disc moved from side to side, and Grale had a sudden disturbing vision of a caterpillar burrowing among mounds of rubbish, and he thought of the picture Sophy had shown him of the infant dreaming in its cocoon. 'What is Man?' the picture had asked, and what was man Grale thought? What was Ferril, and what was he, Hector Grale, and what had brought them to this cellar? Ferril eating the dust of a thousand lies and he, himself, sweating and smelling, lying and grinning. What have we done to deserve this? he thought. We who were once children.

'Well, what have you got?' Ferril demanded.

'It's about Blake,' Grale answered. 'William Blake.'

Ferril went through his ritual with the ledgers. 'Let's have it.'

Grale felt in his pocket for the manuscript of *The French Revolution*. Now that the moment had come he felt a certain reluctance to pass it to Ferril, but he did.

'I went to his house tonight,' Grale said. 'He wasn't in but I had a look round. You said he might be printing sedition, and I found this.' He held up the papers.

Ferril grabbed at them. 'I knew it,' he spat. 'I felt it in my bones. Artists! I tell you, Grale, they used to be respectable people. Why, if you had seen an artist a few years ago you wouldn't have known it. They looked no different from me or — ' he might have been about to say, 'you', but didn't — 'or any other normal person. But look at them now — scum! None of the old ways will do them; oh no, everything's got to be changed, there's no respect for anything any more. I've got my eye on one or two, I can tell you. There's one called Wordsworth who's been in France with the Revolutionaries. He's creeping about England now. If you hear anything about him you let me know. Now, let's have a look at this.'

He unrolled the paper and began to read:

' "The dead brood over Europe: the cloud and vision
    descends over cheerful France;
O cloud well appointed! Sick, sick, the Prince on his
    couch! wreathed in dim
And appalling mist. . ."

'What is this?' Ferril demanded. He flicked over the pages of the manuscript.

' "In the tower nam'd Order, an old man, whose white
    beard cover'd the stone floor like weeds
On margin of the sea. . ."

' "On margin of the sea",' he repeated. 'Why — ' he looked up accusingly — 'this is poetry.'

Grale was apologetic. 'It sounds like it, Sir. He writes poems, and he paints pictures, strange pictures.'

'Do you understand this?' Ferril asked.

'I've not had time to read it, Sir.'

Ferril pored over the poem. ' "And the chamber became as a clouded sky; o'er the Council he stretch'd his red limbs." What does that mean?'

'I don't know.' Grale shook his head. 'I like poetry, Mr. Ferril, but I don't understand this. It sounds violent, though, somehow.'

'Violent, eh? Yes, there's a lot about blood in it, and fire.' Ferril leaned back and sucked his pen. 'It's got to mean something,' he said. 'It stands to reason, a man wouldn't write all this unless it meant something, not unless he was a madman. Do you think that? Is he mad?'

'No, Mr. Ferril.' Grale shook his head. 'His house isn't like a lunatic's house. There is a crazy man lives in my tenement. His room is like a madman's room. Blake's isn't like that.'

Ferril poked at the poem with little nervous, savage jabs, as if it had a life of its own which he wished to destroy.

'What is it all about?' he said. 'What? What?' And then he clicked his fingers. 'Is it a code? It could be — ' His voice rose with excitement. 'It could be. All right, Grale. Stay with Blake. Meet his friends, see if they have any copies of this. We might be on to something. This might be a plot!'

Grale grinned and bowed, echoing Ferril's words in a whisper. 'A plot, yes, a plot.' He took the coin Ferril threw at him and shuffled out. As he closed the door he looked furtively at the coin. It was a guinea. Normally that would have made Grale happy, or as near to happiness as he ever got. But as he trudged through the streets, back to Newgate Street, back to Levant Court, back to his room, and his misery, he felt only a deep and black depression.

Chapter 12

Sophy was asleep when William returned and it was the next morning before she told him of Grale's visit.

'I will call on him,' William said, and after breakfast he set out. It was Sunday, the streets quiet and deserted. But as he walked through the city, church bells began to toll. Disturbed by their clamour, pigeons wheeled through the air, and over St. Clement's a hawk dropped on one and made his breakfast.

As the bells jangled on, people, answering their clamour, shuffled through the barred and bolted streets. William walked through them aloofly until he came to Newgate Street. In a doorway of Levant Court he asked a woman lurking in the shadows where Grale lived.

'Old misery-guts,' she cried. 'Top floor. But what's a nice-looking fellow like you want with the likes of him? I know where we can get a bottle of gin, cheap, have a bit of fun. It's Sunday, isn't it?'

William brushed past her up the squalid stairs. The woman spat and yelled abuse, her screeches mingling with the clamour of the church bells.

On the top floor, tacked to a door, was a grimy notice. 'Hector A. Grale' it said.

William knocked, but there was no answer. He banged again, louder, and a voice asked who was it.

'Blake, William Blake.'

A moment later the door opened and Grale, his shirt hanging outside his trousers, grinned in the doorway.

'Come in, Sir.' Grale gave a feeble imitation of a bow. 'A pleasure, a deep pleasure, to welcome you to my — er living quarters.' He dragged the box forward and rubbed it with his shirt sleeve. 'Forgive my simple arrangements. Temporary, quite temporary.' He paused nervously and stuffed his shirt tails inside his trousers. 'The church bells aroused me just this moment. Do they disturb you, Mr. Blake?'

'No. I am awake before any bells ring.'

'Ah, of course, of course. I am myself. Usually, that is,

usually, you know. Today I have been sleeping in a little. I have not been well. Perhaps Mrs. Blake told you?'

William agreed that she had. 'I hope you are feeling better,' he said.

'Much better.' Actually Grale did not feel better at all, nor did he look it, but he did not wish William to go away. He put on his shoes over bare feet. 'A pleasant sound, the bells, are they not?'

'I do not think so,' William said. 'I have no love of churches, nor the God who is worshipped there.'

'No love of God?' Grale loomed forward, his face like an enormous green moon. 'Are you an atheist, Mr. Blake?'

'You did not hear me aright. I said I had no love for the god worshipped in the churches. What is he but a tyrant, made in the image of a cruel father? I know him too well, say but the wrong word and get a knock on the head. As to God Himself, that is another matter. It is why I have called on you today, to discuss these matters.'

Grale was nervous. 'Of course, of course, that was our agreement. But you must bear with me, Mr. Blake. I am not a clever man — I warned you that I am not clever.'

'That is no matter,' William said. 'I hold no brief for cleverness. Perhaps it is because you are humble that you are enabled to see visions.'

'Visions!' Grale started as if William had said 'A snake'.

'Why yes. Those you talked of at the Swedenborgian Church.' As he spoke, William became aware of a penetrating, vile smell in the room. He moved restlessly. 'Shall we go for a stroll and talk?'

Grale doubted whether he would be able to get down the stairs, but he clapped on his hat and coat. 'Of course, a pleasure indeed.'

He led the way down the stairs and on to the street.

'I thought that we might walk to Spa Fields,' William said. 'The air is clean and I like to listen to the speakers on Sundays. Many fools blabber there, and some rogues, but one hears honest men, now and again.'

Grale was ready to struggle to Spa Fields. Indeed he gave the impression that he was willing to walk to the end of the earth, if William desired it.

'Do not men speak there against the Government?' he asked, in a furtive, confidential manner, as one speaking to an accomplice.

59

'Sometimes that happens,' William agreed, casually. He said no more and the pace he set did not allow Grale to breathe enough to prod him further.

At the large common which was Spa Fields, they halted. Grale took William's arm.

'I would like some breakfast,' he said. 'There is a pie-man over there.'

They went to the hawker and Grale bought a mutton pie and mustard. When he paid, the pie-man snorted with disgust. 'A guinea! I ain't got change for that.'

Grale turned to William who was looking at him thoughtfully. 'Foolish,' he murmured. 'Could you change this for me?'

William shook his head. 'I rarely carry money, Mr. Grale, but if I had in my pocket all I own this morning, I doubt if I could change it.'

Grale mopped his face. 'Of course, of course. It is a large sum. I have an annuity, a legacy from my mother. It is in the funds and I get a guinea or two now and then.'

He returned the pie and began to shamble away.

'What about your breakfast?' William asked. 'We can find change somehow.'

Grale brushed aside the idea. 'Not worth the trouble. I am not hungry, believe me, Sir.' As he spoke a huge rumble echoed from his belly. 'Pardon me, a slight flatulence. Shall we hear the speakers?'

They wandered among the Sunday-morning idlers who had come to listen to, or, more commonly, bait the speakers, who were in full flow. Men warned of the wrath which was to come upon a loose generation, others lamented the nameless sins of an obscure past. One man was telling a sceptical crowd that they were the lost tribe of Israel, another informed two drunken plasterers and their donkey that the Great Pyramid of Giza, rightly understood, contained full and accurate prophecies of every event ever likely to happen in the history of the world.

White-faced and bare-headed, the speakers harangued and pleaded with their listeners with as much passion as if they were asking for mercy before a hanging judge. But not one of them spoke of matters of fact, in all the multitude not one voice was raised about the affairs of the work-a-day world. The spirit reigned over Spa Fields, but it was anyone's guess what the spirit was.

Grale was disappointed. 'There are not so many political speakers as I had hoped for,' he said.

'No. Few men dare to speak their minds about those matters,' William answered. 'Now we are at war with France men are afraid to express their opinions. And where men cannot speak of this world, they turn to the next for consolation. It is safer for them that way. They say that there are spies and such-like dogs who haunt these fields, hoping to hear men condemn themselves out of their own mouths.'

William said this loudly and Grale, absurdly, felt a tremor of fear. He tugged at William's sleeve.

'Perhaps it would be wise to be more discreet,' he muttered, and then wondered why he had said such a thing. Sweat trickled from under the brim of his hat and ran down to his mouth. He tasted its saltiness on his lips and belched again, a huge, windy rumble. 'What have I to be afraid of?' he asked himself. 'I must pull myself together,' and he felt in his pocket for his guinea, as though reaching for a magic talisman.

They came to a halt at the edge of a small crowd. A young man was perched on an old tub. His eyes were raised to the sooty heavens and his arms were folded across his narrow chest.

'Friends,' he was crying, 'do not let Satan fill your hearts. Do not let him feed on your entrails of sin, spare him that feast of your bowels for which he pines. He is with us now, stalking the fields, seeking for his food.'

'He'll be at the pie-stall,' someone yelled. The crowd guffawed and another wit asked whether the Devil ate cats and dogs, then?

'Aye, laugh,' cried the young man. 'Cackle away. In your jeers I hear the cries of the damned, writhing in eternal torture and damnation. And who will laugh then, when you are dragged down into the Pit, when the fire sears your eyeballs, and your ribs are torn out by the demon's claws? Who will laugh when you are cast into the valley of Gehenna, to be gnawed by the worm which dieth not. Will you laugh then?'

He glared around him with red-rimmed eyes and the crowd fell silent before him.

Grale licked his lips. 'This is a little raw for me.'

'Raw it might be,' William said. 'But he speaks the truth as he sees it.'

'But it is not . . . nice, Mr. Blake. This talk of entrails and bowels, it is not polite.'

'Do not be concerned by that,' William said. 'Religion is not a polite thing. Politeness is a way of supressing energy, and energy is religious.'

They strolled away from the speakers and came to a quiet corner by a fallen tree. William sat on the trunk and Grale thankfully collapsed by him.

'It is quite like being in the country,' Grale wheezed. 'Almost rural. Do you like the country, Mr. Blake?'

'Well enough,' William said. 'But it has no special charms for me. Mere seeing is of little value. Rich people run about in their carriages looking at this and that, but what do they gain from it? A man may see the seven wonders of the world and return as ignorant as when he set out. It is the imagination which truly sees, and if we learn to see with our minds then we might see wonders in the meanest street. Boehme, the German cobbler, says that by holding a grain of sand a man can hold eternity in his palm and see infinity. Do you know his writings?'

Grale confessed that he had never heard of him.

'I thought you might,' said William. 'Seeing that you are a

visionary too. You should try reading him. He will reveal a new Heaven — and a new Hell. But I talk too much; I came to hear your views, not to inflict mine.'

'Ah, yes.' Grale writhed. 'I find it difficult to put into words, Mr. Blake. I have told you that I am not clever. The visions come and I see them. That is all.'

'I have told you that there is no need to be concerned with cleverness, Mr. Grale.' William hesitated. 'It is not for me to be your instructor, indeed it may be that I should learn something from you, but it often happens that the truth of what one sees can be distorted by what is already in one's mind. Take that young preacher we heard just now, the Methodist. His vision of Hell is drawn from farthing prints. Such pictures have been used for centuries to frighten people. I do not blame the lad for his language. He has been taught to see that way and so that is the way he sees. Better for him had he never been taught at all, then he might truly have seen Hell, instead of that childish nonsense of pitchforks and men with horns on their heads.' He smiled. 'And now I contradict myself. But yesterday I was with friends and they said that new ways of life demand a new language. I argued against them, but it is true. These men here on these fields know it. They are laughed at by gentlemen and by the mob for their absurdities, but they know in their bones that a new age is here. The pity is, knowing that, they use the old language. It is like pouring new wine into old pots, the stresses are too great and the pots burst. That is what we see on these fields, these deep feelings are too strong for the men who hold them, and they go mad with it. Did they but understand aright they would turn into angels. Your vision interested me because of that — the vision of devils burning old things struck me as true, for devils, rightly understood, are bringers of wisdom. Bitter wisdom maybe, but wisdom nonetheless. Do you understand me?'

Strangely, Grale did. He, too, was the product of change.

For a moment they sat in silence on the tree, then Grale stirred. 'Do you have any friends, Mr. Blake?'

'One or two.' William looked at Grale. 'I think you have not too many friends. You live alone, and that is not good for a man.'

'No, but I am anxious to make acquaintances. I starve for company sometimes. In your house, last night, I was happy then. Mrs. Blake was kind to me.'

63

'Indeed, kindness is her nature,' William said.

'Yes, she showed me your work. You write poetry, Mr. Blake?'

'That is one word for it.'

'I did not fully understand it. It is like. . . like a code almost.' Grale went cold when he said that, and his mouth stretched in its grin.

'Aye.' William's voice had an edge to it. 'Well, perhaps it is. I have been laughed at for it.'

'You have?' Grale was eager. He leaned forward, panting a little. 'I am laughed at, Mr. Blake. The people in Levant Court laugh at me. They tear down my card and write rude words on the door. It is not good to be laughed at. I laugh at nobody, nobody.' He paused, not far from tears.

William sat by him, unmoving, and his stillness calmed Grale.

'I did not always live like this,' he said. 'I have known better things. I had a shop once. It was my father's shop and I inherited it.' As he spoke he wondered why he was telling William these things.

'But you do not have this shop now?'

'No. I went bankrupt. People stopped coming to my shop. I do not think that they liked me, Mr. Blake.'

'What did you sell?' William asked.

'Nails, spades, iron things. I had a man who made them and I sold them in the shop.'

William was silent for a while. He leaned forward and looked at the ground. Leaning forward like that, his head down, he spoke quietly, his voice just carrying to Grale.

'I do not think that your shop failed for that reason, Mr. Grale, because you were not liked. Such things, nails and screws, they are made in the Black Country by machines now and they can be sold cheaply. More cheaply than a man in a shop can make them. You were undersold, Mr. Grale. It happens every day.'

'Oh.' A sour bubble of gas leaked from Grale's lips. 'Oh,' he said.

'It is happening to all of us,' William said. 'Hand-craftsmen, shopkeepers such as you were, weavers and spinners. We are being bound to mechanical wheels and our days of wisdom are spent in drudgery.'

'What am I to do?' Grale asked. 'What can I work at?'

William had no answer. After a moment he rose. 'Come to

my house one day. I will introduce you to my friends.'

'Yes. I will sit here for a while. Thank you.'

'Thank you, Mr. Grale,' William said, and walked away.

He had not gone a yard or two when Grale called to him. 'I am not good, Mr. Blake, I am not a good man.'

William turned and went back. 'Which of us is?' he asked.

Grale shook his head. 'Those demons I told you of. I do not know whether I saw them or whether I made them up.'

'What is the difference?' William asked.

Grale had no reply. William looked down on him for a moment. 'Mr. Grale,' he said, 'you find my poetry obscure but let me tell you a line I have written which you will understand. "Mutual Forgiveness of each vice, such are the Gates of Paradise",'

So saying he turned and walked across the common and was lost to view among the gesticulating orators.

Chapter 13

When William got home he found Ben in the work-room, moodily folding paper. Ben ignored his greeting and hunched over his work, his back bristling with resentment.

William sat down and stretched his legs. 'I spoke sharply to you yesterday,' he said. 'I am sorry for that.'

Ben did not answer. William looked at his stiff back for a moment and smiled. 'I see that you have black days as I do. Well. . .' He shrugged, went to the bench, and picked up a copper plate he had been working on.

'This is nearly finished,' he said. 'But one or two things need doing yet. The sky is a little heavy and the clouds need lightening. Give me the graver.'

Without looking, Ben thrust the tool at William. When he made to take his hand away it was caught in a firm grip.

'Yes,' William said. 'Maybe two or three cuts here, and one or two there, in the corner. That should be enough.'

Ben found his hand, the graver still in it, pressed towards the plate and his wrist being gently turned so that both his hand and the graver were at the correct angle for engraving. William held Ben's hand there for a moment and then released his grasp, leaving just his finger on Ben's wrist.

'Three cuts here, and two there,' William said. 'I think you can see what is wanted.'

'Me?' Ben said.

William appeared not to have heard the question. 'Not deep, nor long. Time to start. This should have been at the Printer's days ago.'

Ben licked his lips. 'Do you mean that?' he asked.

Again William seemed not to have heard the question. But he removed his finger from Ben's hand.

Ben looked at the plate and licked his lips. He knew that it cost money to buy the copper, and that William had spent days cutting it. And he knew, now, that work did not come to William so easily that he could afford to have a plate ruined.

He lifted the graver to the light and looked at its point as he had been taught. The cutting edge glowed like a jewel, as it should if it was ground aright. The light from the point seemed to grow and expand until he thought that he could fall into its aura and be lost there for ever. He would have been happy to stand and stare at it for the rest of the day, and still William made not the slightest movement. Then he lowered the tool – and cut.

'That's all right,' William said. 'Tomorrow we will take this to the Printer. You will make a good engraver. You have the hand, and the eye, and the courage.'

'Courage?' Ben finally looked at William.

'Why, yes. It takes courage to cut straight, and more to try something new.'

Ben looked at the marks he had made, mere scratches on the copper. 'It doesn't seem much.'

William nodded. 'No, but the Chinese say that the journey of a thousand miles begins with a single step.'

He put the plate aside. 'Today I am going to start printing my new book, the *Songs of Experience*. You will help, and it is fitting that you should, for in cutting those marks of your own will, you have tasted experience. The hand of the world is on your shoulder and your days of innocence are over. Make ready.'

From a cupboard he took a slender parcel, wrapped in silk. Inside was a small square of copper and a varnished paper. He looked sombrely at Ben.

'The price of experience is secrets. No other man has ever seen what you are to see. I am going to print a song, one I wrote last night when the world slept. I cannot afford to have my work printed, nor can I afford a type-press of my own, so I use a different method. First I varnish a paper, like this, and then I draw the words and the design on it. Do you see?'

Ben craned forward. On the paper was a delicate white tracery. He peered closer and made out a picture. An aged man, drooping with fatigue and melancholy, was being led by a child through a grim, blank street. Underneath were words, back to front.

'That is the poem,' William said. 'I cannot draw it on the plate direct. If I did, when it was printed the words would come out the wrong way round. But if I put them on in reverse, when I print they come out the right way. Watch!'

With the utmost care he raised the paper and held it poised

over the plate. As he began to lower it the paper trembled. He turned to Ben who was hovering an inch away.

'To do this,' he said, 'we must work miracles. We must cease from breathing!'

Abashed, Ben took a huge breath and held it as William leaned over the plate again, adjusting the paper with meticulous care. Ben's cheeks bulged and his heart pounded. Still William stayed, motionless, over the plate. Ben heard the sea in his ears and stars began to flash before his eyes and still William did not move. And then, as the air began to leak from Ben's lips, William let the paper fall. With a swoop of his hand so fast Ben could scarcely follow it, he swept the paper flat.

Ben let out a gigantic puff of air. 'It's very hard,' he said.

'It is so. But we are not finished yet.' William took the plate, slid it under the press and heaved on the handle. The press came down and clamped the plate. William took a pot and placed it on the fire. Smoke rose from it, filling the room

with a curiously sweet, acrid aroma, like incense. He gave Ben a rod and told him to stir the pot. As Ben did so, William took a glass tank from the cupboard and put it in the sink. Then he filled the tank with a clear liquid from a jar.

After a moment or two he released the press and took the plate out. As deftly as he had laid it on, he stripped the paper from it. A faint spidery scrawl marked the gleaming plate.

'It is good.' William was satisfied. 'Many a time I have

spoiled the work and had to do it again. You have brought me luck, Ben.'

Ben was pleased with the compliment. 'Do you want the graver?' he asked.

William shook his head. He took the pot from the fire and a fine brush.

'This is the wax of bees, Ben. They too work in secret, where no eye can see them.'

He began to paint the letters. Under the wax the words became clear. As he painted, William read the words aloud:

'I wander thro' each charter'd street,
Near where the charter'd Thames doth flow,
And mark in every face I meet
Marks of weakness, marks of woe.

In every cry of every Man,
In every Infant's cry of fear,
In every voice, in every ban,
The mind-forg'd manacles I hear.

How the chimney-sweeper's cry
Every black'ning church appals;
And the hapless soldier's sigh
Runs in blood down palace walls.

But most thro' midnight streets I hear
How the youthful harlot's curse
Blasts the new-born infant's tear,
And blights with plagues the marriage hearse.'

He stretched and turned to Ben. 'Do you know that city?'

'Why,' Ben said wonderingly, 'that man in the bird-market had a mark on his face.'

'Yes.'

'And we saw the convicts with their manacles – ' Ben pointed to the plate. 'It is London!'

'Yes, it is London. But it is any city where men turn away from the truth. It is every city.'

William lifted the plate and held it against the light. 'Yes, the truth has been told. And now we will turn to acid and sulphurous fumes, and burn away the dross, cleansing and purifying, as do the fires of Hell.'

69

He lifted the plate and slid it into the tank. As it went in the acid hissed like a snake and turned into a glistening mass of bubbles. Ben stepped back, alarmed, but William did not move.

'That is acid in the tank,' he said. 'It will burn away the copper but not the wax, so the writing and the picture will be left. Aye, all that is worthless will go, the apparent will be destroyed, the doors of perception will be cleansed, and infinite truths will be revealed.'

Ben was open-mouthed. 'How did you learn this?' he asked.

'Robert, my brother, showed me. He came to me last year when I was in dire need of help. Since he has shown me this truth Sophy and I have earned our living by it, such as it is, printing and selling our books. Otherwise we should have been at the mercy of the booksellers.'

'That was good of him,' Ben said absently. And then something tingled at the back of his mind. 'Last year?' he asked.

'Yes.'

'But I thought — ' Ben put his hand to his mouth. 'I thought that he was dead.'

'Yes, these ten years since. He was a great favourite of mine.' William smiled, and then he saw that Ben's face was white with shock, and his smile vanished.

'It is true, Ben. He came to me in the night and has often done so since. I tell you now for you are a child no longer. When people die they do not necessarily disappear. Love can bring them back, as maybe hate can.' He put his hand on Ben's shoulder. 'You will not see him, but if you cannot bear that knowledge then get you to Godwin. He would be glad to take you in and teach you on the most truly rational lines. He thinks that he is a man of reason, although he believes in more marvels than a nun.'

As casually as if he were discussing the weather he turned and began wrapping the plate Ben had just cut.

Ben shrugged. After a moment he said, 'That man was here the other night.'

'Which man is that?'

'The one we saw at the meeting. The man who kept grinning.'

'Mr. Grale? I know. Sophy told me.'

'I don't like him,' Ben said. 'He's like old Carlin.'

'Carlin?' William raised an eyebrow.

'The man I used to work for.' Ben was testy at William's forgetfulness. 'The candle-maker. He used to grin all the time when there was anyone about. Then when they had gone he used to kick us kids.'

'I see.' William nodded. 'And you think Mr. Grale is like that, do you?'

'Yes, I do,' Ben said bluntly.

'Aye?' William carefully tied the parcel. 'Let me tell you something, Ben. When I was a lad, working for Basire, the engraver, I knew a man called Stanton. He was what you might call a good man. Everyone said so. But I was a watchful lad, as you are, and I was a sceptical lad at times, like you, and I watched this good man. And he was good. He was kind to his friends and to strangers. He told the truth and he paid his bills, he feared God and honoured the King. But there was something rotten at his core, something like a blind worm lived at the heart of his soul. One day it rose from the darkness and I saw it behind his eyes. I, and I alone, saw it. A year later he was caught and hanged for attacking a child. He had done it for many years.'

'I'm not talking about good men,' Ben protested. 'I'm talking about Grale.'

'Yes,' William said. 'And Mr. Grale is black and greasy. His clothes are dirty and so is his skin, and so too, I have no doubt, is his mind. Look deep, and deeper, and deeper still, and you will find nothing but blackness and wretchedness. But what if there is something at the heart of that man which is good, as there was something at Stanton's heart which was foul. What then?'

'I don't know,' Ben said. 'But Sophy told me that it is wrong to steal.'

'Why, so it is.'

'Well, Grale steals,' Ben said. 'When he was here he took something — some paper. I saw him. He thought no one was looking but I was.'

William frowned. 'Paper, you say? Well, we can spare a bit of paper, I think. A poor man might need some and and be ashamed to ask for it.'

'It wasn't just paper,' Ben insisted. 'It had writing on it. He looked at it before he stuck it in his pocket.'

'Well, it is possibly a poem he took to read. I will ask Sophy if there is anything missing. Maybe I will ask the man himself. But for now we will leave it.'

He left the room leaving Ben by the tank. Ben peered into the acid. It was strange, he thought, that as he sat watching and the world went on about its affairs, the acid was eating away at the copper, secretly, silently, revealing the words and the designs of William Blake.

What other mysteries were there in the world, he wondered. What other burning and corrosion was taking place, wiping clean and purifying; and what would be revealed when the cleansing fires had done their work?

Chapter 14

It was after twelve the next day before William set off for the Printer's with the plate Ben had helped to engrave. To Ben's disappointment the handing over of the engraving was quick and business-like. A man in a dirty apron tilted the plate to the light, pulled his mouth down, said it would do, in a manner which suggested that if it did it was because of his forbearance rather than William's skill, handed over some money, and waved them out. He did not give William any further work.

The way from the Printer's led William and Ben through Whitehall, past the great offices of the Government. Ben was impressed by the buildings, and by their guards who marched up and down the courtyards glittering in brass and steel. But William was scornful.

'Donkeys are dressed up on May Day, but they are donkeys just the same,' he said, and walked on with his determined tread.

Ben followed him, but as they turned into Westminster he turned and looked up at the windows high on the buildings. Just briefly he wondered who worked up there, commanding the pomp and glory of the soldiers.

And as Ben was looking up, a man was looking down on the street. He saw Ben and felt a mild, civilized pleasure at the sight of the boy, so neat and nimble, and so obviously enjoying the sights around him. A charming boy, he thought, and turned reluctantly to the man in green who stood before his desk, droning out a long report.

'. . . Agent Number 22 saw one Joseph Garrold talking to one John Thelwall in the White Boar. Said Thelwall had a copy of *The Rights of Man* and was urging Garrold to speak against the Government amongst the Journeyman Tailors. Paid said agent one guinea. Agent Number 17 attended a meeting of bricklayers in the Red Lion tavern. Said bricklayers drank to Liberty and Free Speech. Paid said agent five shillings.'

The man at the window yawned and stuffed his hands in his coat pocket. At last the speaker came to an end.

'That is all, my Lord. If you would sign here.'

The man leaned forward and glanced at the total of the long list of payments. 'Ninety-two guineas, thirteen shillings, and five pence — and a farthing. You are most meticulous, Ferril,' he said, and scrawled his signature, 'Braxton'.

'Is that all?' he asked.

'Just one more thing, my Lord.' Ferril took out *The French Revolution* and laid it on the table. 'An informer brought this in.'

Braxton yawned again. 'What is it?'

Ferril looked embarrassed. 'I don't rightly know, my Lord. It looks as if it might be a poem — like Shakespeare, Sir, but I don't understand it. I thought you might tell me what it means. I know you like poetry, my Lord.'

'Do you indeed?' Braxton looked sharply at Ferril. 'You know a great many things, Mr. Ferril.' He walked to his desk and sat down: a long elegant figure in maroon and white; charming, sceptical, balanced. 'And who wrote this mysterious effusion?'

'A man called William Blake, Sir.'

'Do I know this Blake?'

'No, my Lord. But I do. He is an engraver and I like to keep an eye on anyone who has access to printing presses.'

'Very wise, I am sure.' Braxton poked at the document. 'William Blake, it is a very English name.'

'Yes, my Lord. He is an Englishman. Respectable parents. His father was a hosier in Soho. Blake went to Pars's Drawing School and the Royal Academy. He learned his craft from Basire, the engraver. Now he does journeyman work when he can get it.'

'Associates?'

'Yes. He knows many bad elements in the town. He knows Johnson, who was going to print *The Rights of Man* before we frightened him off.'

'That book!' Braxton's poise slipped a little. 'That book is a curse, a curse. Every mechanic has a copy in his pocket. Who would have thought that a corset-maker would have such an effect on the world.' He rose and stalked to the window. 'A corset-maker, can you imagine a more degrading occupation?'

Ferril could think of hundreds but he did not say so.

Braxton turned, scowling. 'It was you who let Paine slip through our fingers, was it not?'

'That wasn't my fault, my Lord.' Ferril was unperturbed. 'The warrant was out, the constables were at his house. . .' He shrugged. 'But I know one thing, my Lord.'

'And what is that?'

'The night he slipped away to France he had dinner with Johnson — and he was told to go on the run.'

'Yes?'

'William Blake told him that, my Lord.'

'Did he now, did he now?' Braxton tapped on the window. 'I should have known that you would have a little something up your sleeve, Mr. Ferril. I will read this poem and let you know my views. These men, Mr. Ferril — Godwin, Johnson, Paine, this Blake, Thelwall, and all the rest of the rabble-rousers — they prate of free speech and liberty, and their rights under the Constitution, but there is no Constitution, and they have no rights. And the rod to teach them that lesson is being prepared now. You have a man watching this Blake?'

'Yes.'

'What is he?'

'A failed shopkeeper.'

'A failure? Is such a man right for this work?'

Ferril did not say that failures were the only people who would do the work. Not that it mattered. 'They are the best,' he said simply. 'It gives them something to hate, gives them an appetite for their work, you might say.'

'Well,' Braxton nodded, 'we must leave it in your hands, Mr. Ferril. You say that this Blake was at the Royal Academy?'

Ferril agreed that he had said so, received a wave of the hand, and bowed himself out.

When he had gone, Braxton settled down in his chair, swung his long legs onto the table, and began to read *The French Revolution*. He read for an hour, frowning over the pages, and then, as dusk thickened among the spires of London's churches, he locked the pages in his desk and left the building.

He strolled across Whitehall and ambled through the mists of the river, down the Strand to Somerset House, into the Royal Academy. Students, clutching their portfolios, were leaving the studios, and porters were lighting the lamps in the courtyards. Braxton received the salutes due to him as a patron of the Academy and went inside. Braxton liked the Academy. He liked the quiet concentration of the studios, the smell of paint, the young and earnest men intent upon the study of the Masters of the past. It was work, but work lacking the vulgarity of the shop or factory.

He liked, too, the members' sitting-room. Unlike the cramped studios, it was spacious, and had a sober comfort which appealed to him. And the members were interesting. They were, when all was said and done, merely craftsmen, intrinsically of no more merit than tailors, yet they were all well-mannered and knew the world — and, of course, their place in it. But with it all, there was something about them which inspired a flicker of respect. Perhaps, Braxton thought, it was the ability to create something from nothing. Not many men could do that.

Tonight, as Braxton entered the room, there were a group of men standing by the fire. One of them, a small man in a sparkling wig, caught sight of Braxton and waved to him. Braxton made his way across the room.

'Mr. Gore.' He bowed.

'Lord Braxton.' Gore bowed in return, more deeply. 'You may know these gentlemen — ' he waved his hand — 'and they, I am sure, know of you. Lord Braxton is a member of the Government,' he announced. 'Our destinies are in his hands.'

'I think the Prime Minister would raise an eyebrow at that,' Braxton said. 'I am the most junior of clerks. I read a little for the Government now and then.'

There were suitable smiles at this modest sally. One of the group asked how the war with France was going.

'Well enough,' Braxton said. 'We have gallant soldiers, a determined Government, and the Navy. And we have the will to carry on the struggle.'

'Here, here,' cried the man. 'Tell Mr. Pitt, Sir, that we are all with him in the war. Every inch of the way. The French are madmen, madmen. Barras, Robespierre — mark my words, they will bring France to ruin — and Europe, too, unless they are stopped. Every rascal in Europe is infected with their ideas — what do they call 'em? Liberty, Equality, Fraternity — preposterous nonsense. What does it all mean but that Jack's as good as his master? Stop them, Sir, stop them.'

76

Gore intervened. 'I am sure that his Lordship and the Government will. But you did not come here to talk of the war, I think, my Lord. Will you not join me in opening a bottle of claret? I see the Master of Drawing. . .'

He politely disengaged Braxton from the company and led him across the room to a large divan. Here a man was sitting reading a newspaper.

'Moser,' Gore said, 'make room for us.'

The Master of Drawing was ready enough to do that. A servant appeared with a decanter and glasses, and when the drinks had been poured and healths drunk, the three men leaned back with an air of leisured confidence.

'And how are your students, Mr. Moser?' Braxton asked. 'Have we any rising young men?'

'Well, my Lord,' Moser said judiciously. 'We are never without talent, I trust. . . has a fine eye, a very fine eye, and. . . is as good a colourist as any in Europe, I dare say. Your Lordship is thinking of adding to your collection?' He cocked an eye at Braxton who smiled.

'I am always interested in new talent, I hope.'

'Well, my Lord, landscape, historical, portrait – I think we can accommodate you. The British artist is as good as any other, and better than most.'

'Ah.' Braxton swished his claret around his glass. 'But are all your pupils swans? Do you have no geese?'

'Yes, indeed,' Moser said. 'It does not do to expect too much, and why should we? A cabinet-maker's apprentices are not all Sheratons – why should all ours be Gainsboroughs or Van Dykes? But even the geese do, my Lord. There is a demand for Drawing Teachers, Decorators. . . yes.' He drank his claret as if drinking a toast to the geese of the art world.

Braxton drank too.

'But do not some of your eggs fail to hatch at all?'

The Master of Drawing blew out his cheeks and Gore pursed his lips in an offended way. But Braxton was undeterred.

'Did I not hear of one such the other day?' he said smoothly. 'A William Hake – or Rake?'

'Blake!' the Master of Drawing cried. 'William Blake! Pray, my Lord, do not mention that man to me.' He shuddered as if at the memory of some frightful experience. 'Gore, tell Lord Braxton of the man.'

Gore smiled ruefully. 'He was a student here for a while, my Lord, but we have never had one like him before nor since, thank heaven. He refused to draw from the life, or to copy any living thing at all. He said that the Goths were great painters — the Goths! — barbarous monks in the Middle Ages. He said that he could see ghosts and spirits and he said that Sir Joshua could not paint — Sir Joshua Reynolds, Sir! I could go on.' He shook his head. 'He would go his own way without regard to rhyme or reason.'

Braxton smiled and waved the waiter to bring another bottle of claret. 'This Blake sounds a regular enthusiast,' he said.

Moser was agitated. 'The word exactly, my Lord. An Enthusiast. All that mattered to him was his own feelings. He was like, like. . .' He searched for a word which would express his feelings. 'Like a preacher, my Lord. A preacher in Cromwell's army. A fanatic. . . there.' He sank back into the divan.

'Did he have talent?' Braxton asked.

'Talent, Sir? What has talent to do with it? What is the use of talent if a man will not learn the rules of art? It is like a Government without the Peerage, if your Lordship will pardon the allusion. Am I not right, Gore?'

'Of course,' Gore agreed. 'But there is the man to tell you of Blake, my Lord.' He pointed to the door where a solid-looking man had entered.

'That is Flaxman, the sculptor. I believe he is a friend of Blake's. Would you care to meet him, my Lord?'

Braxton did care and Flaxman was beckoned over and introduced. At Braxton's name he bowed, formally, and clearly expected the bow to be returned.

'Crack a bottle with us, Flaxman,' Moser said. 'We were just talking of your William Blake.'

'My Blake?' Flaxman raised his eyebrows. 'You have the wrong word there, Moser. Blake is his own man, none more so in all London. But how come that you were talking of him?'

'His name came up,' Braxton said, smoothly. 'We were talking of rising men. I might say that you could have been mentioned there.'

Flaxman deflected the compliment. 'My talents are not of the greatest.'

'I know that not to be true,' Braxton said. 'But this Blake

79

seems a strange fellow.'

'Strange?' Flaxman spread his blunt hands. 'I believe Michael Angelo was thought so too, in his time.'

'Then you do not think that this man is crazy?' Braxton asked.

'No, my Lord. I do not.'

'Mr. Flaxman!' Gore gave a horrified cry. 'Blake says that he saw the Prophet Elijah up a tree on Clapham Common. I heard it with my own ears.'

'Well, as to that, when I stand before a block of marble do I not see a vision of what I am to carve? What is the difference between that and Blake's visions? We all have our visions, do we not, my Lord?' He turned and faced Braxton.

Braxton's face was quizzical, good-humoured. 'I trust that my visions are not so original, nor do I see them up trees on Clapham Common.'

'No more do you, Mr. Flaxman,' Gore said.

'No, Sir,' Flaxman said. 'But then I am not a man of genius.'

'You used that word, genius?' Braxton said.

'I do.' Flaxman was firm. 'We are all such jolly good fellows here in the Academy. We know the rules and abide by them. Trust us not to do anything which is not correct. We know what goes on in each other's minds — and there is nothing there to disturb us. But who knows what is going on in Blake's mind?'

'I'll warrant he doesn't know himself,' Gore said. 'Have you seen his paintings? Lunacy — mere lunacy. How can you justify them, Flaxman?'

'Not by any rules that I know of,' Flaxman said. 'But perhaps that says something about the rules of art rather than about William Blake.'

'You do not agree with the rules, Mr. Flaxman?' Braxton asked.

'It is no matter whether I do or don't,' said Flaxman. 'But if the rules cease to have meaning or relevance, then they will go. Indeed, I believe that they are going, gentlemen. Men like Cowper the poet, or Bowles, they strike a new note in poetry, so the young men tell me, and they are imitated. To be sure, who writes like Pope these days?' Flaxman drank and Braxton refilled his glass.

'Thank you, my Lord. Do you dance?' Flaxman asked.

'Dance?' Braxton smiled. 'If a gun is placed at my head, I might.'

80

'I too,' Flaxman said. 'But tonight I am going to a Ball at Holland House and I shall sit and watch the dancing. It is pleasant to watch; the Minuet and the Gavotte — all so stately and ordered. I have thought that it is like an image of our society, everyone knowing the rules — and abiding by them. Rules and harmony, harmony and rules. But in Paris, Sir, in Paris, they are dancing a German measure called the waltz. Men and women dance together, apart from the rest. They hold each other by the waist and dance intimately. It is quite shocking, I believe. And the social order has quite gone from it. It is a trivial detail but the first drop of rain presages a storm.'

'You are not an admirer of these changes are you, Flaxman,' Moser asked.

'I am a describer, Sir,' Flaxman answered. 'But I tell you this, when the Bastille fell it was not only the prisoners inside it who were released, but a new spirit.'

'A spirit of violence,' Braxton said sharply.

'That may be, and I am no admirer of force, whoever uses it. I am not the judge of the world, nor are any of us, but it seems to me that a door in history is opening, and it is men like Blake who are opening it. And none of us will close it again, whether for good or evil.'

'Upon my soul,' Braxton said. 'You make me feel that obscurity can be quite dangerous.'

'We could agree there,' Flaxman answered. 'Was there ever a more dangerous tune than the Marseillaise, and yet do you know the composer? And was there ever a man more obscure in his time than Jesus Christ?'

There was a slightly embarrassed pause, as if, by mentioning Christ, Flaxman had been guilty of a breach of manners. Then Gore coughed.

'Well, my Lord, you have had quite an art lesson.'

'Oh yes.' Braxton smiled benignly and rose. 'It will add to my pleasures. I collect a little, you know.'

Moser raised his hand anxiously. 'I trust you take outdoor pleasures, my Lord. It does not do to over-tax the mind.'

'Yes.' Braxton nodded his appreciation of Moser's concern. 'I hunt a little you know. Yes, I hunt.'

Chapter 15

Flaxman went to his Ball at Holland House but the dancers, moving in their elegant files, were not his interest. For a long time he sat talking quietly to a harsh-faced man. As the man spoke, Flaxman's face creased in a frown, and he left the Ball early.

The next morning he walked over to Lambeth, to Hercules Buildings. With the easy air of a guest certain of his welcome, he strolled round the back of the Blakes' house and entered the kitchen. Sophy was at the table, her arms white with flour, but she greeted Flaxman without embarrassment, as one worker to another.

'You look like a sculptor, Sophy, dusted white like that,' Flaxman said.

Sophy smiled. 'I'm making a pudding,' she said.

Flaxman bent over the dish. 'That has more of art than many a sculpture I have seen,' he said. 'Is William in?'

'Yes, he is in the work-room. He will be glad to see you.'

Flaxman hesitated. 'Is he working?'

In her turn Sophy hesitated too. 'Yes. . . on his own book.'

'I see.' Flaxman nodded and left the kitchen.

As he entered the work-room, William's eyes lit up. 'John,' he cried. 'It is good to see you.' He seized Flaxman's arm. 'As solid as ever. It is easy to tell when a sculptor is working, eh?'

'Well, the commissions do come,' Flaxman said. 'With all this new building there is a demand for sculpture. The Antique figure is all the rage and the builders seem to have decided that I can carve it.' He shrugged as if disclaiming the responsibility.

'Ah.' William patted Flaxman on the back. 'Take your work, John. You will make something decent of it. Yes.' His face glowed as he spoke.

'You are too generous, William.' Flaxman caught sight of Ben in a corner by the sink. 'And this is?'

William slapped his thigh. 'Ah, you have made me forget my manners!' He pulled Ben from his corner. 'I could say that this lad is my apprentice, but he is the third of our family. Ben, this is John Flaxman. He is a sculptor and a good one. And a good man.'

Flaxman winked at Ben. 'Don't believe everything a poet tells you, Ben. They are wild fellows.'

He held out his hand, and Ben, somewhat timidly, shook it, and was taken aback by its power.

'It is always my pleasure to meet a fellow craftsman,' Flaxman said. 'How do you like engraving?'

Ben muttered that he liked it very much. Flaxman grinned. 'The first year or so is the worst. I remember the first time I cut a block of marble. I was so nervous I almost fainted. I had to go for a walk afterwards.'

'I felt like that,' Ben said with deep feeling.

'You will learn. The material will teach you.' Flaxman turned to William. 'I had heard about your lad. A day or so ago I called on Godwin.'

A little of the good humour faded from William's face. 'Oh yes? Did he mention my pictures? I showed him one or two when I was there last.'

'He mentioned them,' Flaxman admitted.

'I can guess what he said.' William frowned heavily and

half-closed his eyes. 'Poor Blake, such talent — but all wasted on dreams and delusions. His sympathetic nerves have been quite distorted. I despair of him, yes, despair.'

It was a surprisingly good impersonation of Godwin and Ben laughed as heartily as Flaxman. When the laughter had died down, Flaxman shook his head.

'Come now, William, do not be too hard on Godwin. He has spoken out for freedom, you know.'

'That I do not deny,' William answered. 'But he and his kind might end up greater enemies than our rulers. Pitt and the rest of them, they will die, and what they represent will die with them, but ideas have a habit of lingering. And I tell you, Godwin's ideas are dangerous. They are the concepts of the counting-house. "Add up the facts and you understand all!" that teaches us to worship man — and what can be more dangerous than that?'

'Well, leave it there, William,' Flaxman said easily. 'I did not come to talk about Godwin. Let me see your new work.'

Somewhat unwillingly, William wrenched his mind from Godwin and for an hour or so he and Flaxman looked at the pictures for the *Songs of Experience*.

At length, Flaxman raised his head and sighed. William anticipated his words. With a touch of bitterness he said, 'Say it, John. Ask me why I cannot make my work clear so that any numbskull can understand it.'

'Why,' Flaxman looked at William through his steady eyes, 'I was about to ask when the world would grow to understand you. It is we who must grow up, not you who must speak down.'

William ducked his head in a stiff bow. 'Forgive me, John. I speak a little too sharply at times.'

'We all do that.' Flaxman waved the incident aside. He paused, then, carefully picking his words, he said:

'I was at the Academy last night. Your name was mentioned.'

'What were they proposing? To hang me?'

Flaxman gave a rather forced laugh. 'Not quite that, I think.'

'Who was there?'

'Oh. Moser, Gore. . .'

'That pair?' William was contemptuous. 'They know less of art than two chimney-sweeps.'

'Yes. There was another there.'

84

'Oh?' The tone of Flaxman's voice drew William's attention. 'Who might that have been?'

'A nobleman. A member of the Government. One Lord Braxton. He had a deal to ask about you, William.'

William flicked his engraver's wheel and watched it spin round. 'Why should such a man ask about me?'

Flaxman coughed. 'He is a Patron of the Academy. I am told that he collects works of art.'

'Not mine.' William was dismissive.

'Yes, I will confess that seems unlikely. Which made me wonder why he should be so interested in you.'

The wheel was slowing down. William waited until it stopped. 'Yes?'

'I was at Holland House last night. I heard a little about Lord Braxton — and his job.'

'And that is?' William spoke as if he would not be surprised at the answer no matter what it was.

'He is a secretary at the Home Office. He deals with correspondence for the Prime Minister.' Flaxman folded his arms. 'But that, it seems, is only one of his tasks. It seems that he is also concerned with. . . sedition.'

'Sedition?' William frowned.

Flaxman was uncomfortable. 'So I was told, and my authority was good. It could be a coincidence, of course.'

'I do not believe in such coincidences,' William said flatly.

'Nor do I,' Flaxman agreed. 'Which is why I have told you.'

There was a grim silence. Flaxman looked carefully away from William.

'Last night Braxton spoke about the French Revolution. I tell you, William, they can smell revolution in the air in Whitehall, and they can hear the French drums in Downing Street. I think that the time is coming when Pitt will take off his gloves when he deals with those he thinks a danger to the existing order. That is merely my opinion.' Picking his words, he said slowly, 'It is what I would say to a man who might be threatened, were I to know such a man, that is.'

'Aye?' William was curt. 'Well, I have nothing to do with politics now. I have left all that behind me.'

'Come now, William.' Flaxman was slightly impatient. 'But a minute ago you said that Godwin was a danger because of his ideas. How much more so is a man who can express his thoughts in songs and pictures? And you say yourself that your work is revolutionary.'

William's face was dark with blood. 'My pictures and songs? Do not tell me Pitt is afraid of those. Not fifty men have read them. In any case, the revolution I speak of is a revolution of the soul.'

Flaxman shrugged helplessly. 'You may find men like Braxton not so ready with fine distinctions. I thought I would mention it, that is all. Well, they say that in Cathay if a man brings bad tidings his head is chopped off.' He took his hat. 'I must go, William. I have an engagement. I had no wish to upset you.'

'No.' William's answer was flat and ungracious but Flaxman took it gently. He rested his hand on William's shoulder, shook hands with Ben, and left.

After a moment's indecision, Ben turned back to his work. He was colouring a song but he could not concentrate. After a while he peered over his shoulder at William. He was scowling through the window. Ben had never seen him looking so black and it was with relief that he heard Sophy's footsteps in the hall.

She came into the room, her sleeves rolled up. 'I asked John to stay for his dinner but he could not. There is a man I am always glad to see. . .' Her voice died away as she saw the expression on William's face. She raised her eyebrows at Ben who shrugged and held out his hands.

'What's the matter, William?' Sophy asked. 'Is anything wrong?'

William did not answer for a moment, then he swung round. 'Wrong?' he cried. 'When is there anything right? Is it not enough that the booksellers will not stock my books, or that any hack who licks the carpet at the Academy can smirk at me — is that not enough. Do I have to be spied on now?'

'William — ' Sophy was bewildered. 'What is this about spying?'

'Flaxman has just told me. A creature called Lord Braxton has been snooping after me.'

For one second Sophy's eyes lit up. She opened her mouth but with a slashing movement of his arm William cut off her words.

'He is not going to buy my work. Let us have no delusions, spare me those.'

'But why — why should this Lord ask about you? I don't understand,' Sophy said.

86

'Because he is a dog paid to sniff out those Pitt calls traitors, and he considers me one.'

'But you are not a traitor,' Sophy said. 'You will not even listen to talk of politics now. Why should this man bother you?'

'Because I speak my mind,' William said bitterly.

Sophy could hardly believe her ears. 'You are entitled to your beliefs.'

'Entitled!' William slammed his fist on the bench. 'This Government will hang men for believing in Jesus Christ if it suits them. What Flaxman said is true. Sedition is in the air. Every workman in England knows that the French killed their masters. It has happened there, why not here? Pitt knows that, every man in England goes to bed with that thought in his head.'

'But you never talk of these things.' Sophy was frightened, and her fear showed in her voice. Ben was frightened, too. He shrank into a corner, appalled at the talk of hanging. But William had not finished.

'A man does not need to talk of political matters to be a threat in times like these. If a free man speaks his mind without fear, that is political, even though he speaks of the weather.'

'I see.' Sophy had tears in her eyes. There were some papers on the floor and she knelt and gathered them together. On her knees she held them up to William. He took them, then threw them back to the floor.

'Damn the books,' he cried. 'Damn them, damn them all.' He moved his hands before his eyes in a queer gesture, like a man brushing away cobwebs, and strode from the room. A moment later the door slammed.

Sophy screwed her apron in her hands, but forced a smile.

'We seem to be short of good news these days,' she said. 'But never fear. Why, this is probably all a mistake. It may be that this Lord wants to buy William's work.'

She forced a smile but her lips were trembling. She turned away. 'Why,' she said, her voice muffled, 'how could anyone be so foolish as to think William a danger?' And then she was crying.

Ben was not far from tears himself. As much as anything he would have liked to run forward and bury his head against Sophy and blubber. Instead he walked forward and put his arm on her shoulder.

'Yes,' he said. 'It will be all right, Sophy.' As he spoke he was surprised at his own steadiness. Even as he comforted Sophy the thought flashed through his mind that he was growing up.

He patted Sophy and she shook her head. 'I'm all right, Ben, truly I am. There.' She wiped her eyes on her apron. 'Go to William, Ben. He is on his own and needs you.'

Ben frowned but Sophy was insistent. 'He does, he has had enough blows these past days. Show him that there is someone who is staunch. Go.'

She knelt again and began picking up the papers, and Ben, after a moment looking at her, turned and left the house.

Chapter 16

Ben wandered down the street but there was no sign of William. He leaned on the bridge. Across the river, like a fortress behind its moat, the city sprawled, brooding and sullen beneath a leaden sky. Under the bridge the river sucked at the buttresses as the tide turned. A thin wind blew, icy against Ben's cheek. He shivered and turned up his coat collar, but still he dawdled, listening to the evil gurgle of the water. Winter was coming, he thought, already it was cold enough for snow.

At last he turned and went back along the street. He walked past Hercules Buildings and went on to where the street narrowed into a muddy lane which ran through market gardens and drab, marshy fields. Across a meadow he saw a flicker of blue. He hurried forward and found William looking into a hedge.

As Ben came up to him, William nodded absently, aware of his presence. Ben looked over his shoulder. In the dark recesses of the hedge, purple brambles coiled among the hawthorn and among them briars hooked their thorns. Sheltered by the hedge the briars still held a few wilted dog-roses, their petals brown with autumn's rot.

William carefully pulled a rose free and sat down on the bank. Ben sat next to him. William turned the rose in his fingers. Even that slight movement disturbed it and mildewed petals eddied to the ground, revealing the black pistil.

William pointed to it. 'Do you see that dark secret?' he asked.

Ben could not see any secrets, dark or otherwise, only the rotten stub of a flower. And it occurred to him that he had heard enough about secrets, dark or otherwise.

'Sophy is crying,' he said.

'Yes.' William's voice was calm. 'Yes.' He leaned back into the hedge, his red hair framed by its subtle greens and browns.

'Don't you care?' Ben demanded.

'That Sophy is crying? Oh yes, I care about that, Ben. More than you know, perhaps. But I feel more sorrow for those who have never known tears.'

Since he had known William, Ben had felt many emotions. Now, for the first time, he felt a prickle of dislike. William touched the flower again.

'I thought once that what I could see would be clear to anyone, if they but desired to see it. Now I am no longer sure.'

Ben scowled. 'Aren't you worried?'

'About Sophy?'

'About everything.' Ben was impatient.

'No.'

Ben blinked. 'You're not? What about this Lord Mr. Flaxman talked about?'

'What of him?' William asked.

'Well — ' Ben was angry. 'You were talking about being hanged just now. That's why Sophy is crying.'

William shook his head. 'I wasn't worried. I was angry.'

Ben snatched at a handful of grass. 'What's the difference?'

'Anger is health, worry is disease. I am not diseased. But I will tell you this. I have spent twenty years of my life writing, and every line has been written so that men will know the truth about themselves. Now it seems that they do not even know the truth about me.'

'Well.' Ben was dogged. 'What are you going to do about it?'

William smiled. 'What should I do?'

'You can find out why they are after you. Someone has told them about you. Find him.'

'Who is there to find? I have no enemies.'

'Godwin doesn't like you,' Ben said.

'Perhaps not,' William agreed. 'But that is not to be thought of. He is a man of honour.'

'Well, I'll bet I know who it is.' Ben was venomous. 'It's that Grale. He's no good. I've told you that before, but you wouldn't listen.'

'Grale?' William was grave. 'That's a hateful thought to me, Ben. I would that you had said any other name.'

'Why? Why are you so soft about Grale?' Ben was exasperated.

'Because he is a solitary being, Ben. Suppose Godwin were to betray a man. I could understand that for it would be for some great purpose, something he conceived greater than any one man. But Grale; there is a man without friends, without a home, perhaps without beliefs if what you say is true. His life is more worthless than a stray dog's. What would such a man sell me for but money? And who would put himself in the chair of Judas Iscariot unless despair drove him to it? And if he does despair then it is because I have betrayed him worse. But I cannot believe it. What could he say about me but lies easily disproved? Men like this Lord Braxton have more to do than waste their time on shoddy fables.'

Ben pulled his face. 'That's just talk,' he said. 'He stole that paper.'

William dropped the rose-stem and turned to face Ben.

'Why, so he did. I had forgotten that. You have an eye for fact, Ben.'

'Right.' Ben jumped to his feet. 'Let's go and get him.'

William frowned. 'Get him?'

'That's right. We'll go to his house and beat him up.'

'And what good will that do?'

'He won't spy again,' Ben said flatly.

'Perhaps it is why he did it this time.' William stood up. 'But it is not Grale I am concerned about, nor even Lord Braxton. There is a sickness at the heart of England, these things are but symptoms.'

He turned and walked down the lane. Ben followed him moodily.

'You were ready to hit that man in the bird-market,' he shouted.

William spoke over his shoulder. 'They were attacking an innocent creature.'

'Well, you're being attacked,' Ben said.

'Yes.' William turned, his eyes glinting. 'But I am not innocent.'

There was a bite in William's voice which silenced Ben and they walked on to Hercules Buildings in silence.

They turned into the house and went to the parlour. At the door they halted, surprised. A man was standing before the fire talking to Sophy.

Sophy, too, had found it hard to stay in the house. After Ben left, she wrapped her shawl around herself and went out. She had no clear idea of where she was going. She walked across the bridge, her face clouded and sad.

As she walked by the river she heard her name being

called. When she turned she saw a man across the street,
waving. He dodged a heavy dray and approached her, raising
his hat.

'It is Mrs. Blake, is it not?' The man asked.

Sophy backed away and the man smiled.

'Butts, Ma'am, Mr. Butts. We met at Mr. Godwin's house
some weeks ago.'

'I remember,' Sophy agreed.

'I was on my way to your house,' Butts said. 'I was hoping
to speak to Mr. Blake.' He looked sharply at Sophy. 'Excuse
me, is anything wrong?'

His voice was firm but concerned. Sophy's eyes filled with
tears and she took out her handkerchief and blew her nose
vigorously.'

'There has been. . . please forgive me. . .'

Butts raised his hand. 'I do not wish to intrude, Mrs. Blake.
If it is anything personal. . .' He spoke with surprising
delicacy for such a blunt-looking man.

Sophy dabbed at her eyes. 'No, it is not anything like that.' She looked at Butts' candid face, as open as her own. 'William is in trouble. He is being spied on by the Government.'

Butts was staggered. 'Spied on!'

'Yes.' Sophy told Butts of the morning's happenings. When she had finished, Butts' face was stern. 'Monstrous,' he said. 'Quite monstrous.' He muttered something to himself which Sophy did not quite catch then cleared his throat. 'May I accompany you home, Ma'am. This makes me more anxious to see Mr. Blake.'

Sophy had no objection and they walked back to Hercules Buildings together.

Ben was enormously pleased to see Butts. The presence of another man, and a straightforward one, who had not come to bring bad news, seemed to lift a huge burden from his shoulders, and from Sophy's too. William, though, was unmoved. He was not aggressively impolite but after a nod at Butts he settled in his chair and stared at the fire, as though nothing existed beyond its flames.

Butts did not seem perturbed by this. He found a chair and drank a glass of milk, admired the room and the cat, asked Ben how he liked the engraving craft, and thought that the milk was better than that his dairyman provided.

'It is because you live so near the country, I dare say,' he said. 'Your cows live in the fields and eat sweet grass. I think that mine is penned in a cellar and is fed on old clothes. I have thought of living near the country but my work keeps me in the city.'

'And what is that?' Sophy asked.

'Why, Ma'am.' Butts put down his glass and wiped his lips on a lawn handkerchief. 'Why, Ma'am, I work for the Government.'

Sophy was startled and William turned from the fire.

'Men from the Government are not welcome here today,' he growled.

'No.' Butts raised his hand. 'I can well understand that, Mr. Blake. But my job is a humdrum one. I do no more than count the country's monies. Still, if my presence offends you —'

He stood up but William waved him down. Quite equably, Butts took his seat again.

'Why did you come here?' William asked.

Butts leaned forward. 'Because I wanted to see more of

your work, Mr. Blake. You were a little sharp with me at Godwin's; well, I understand that. I suppose that you thought I was not paying attention. But the atmosphere at Godwin's was not cordial, and I am a slow man; I like to think and I do not jump to conclusions. So, if you will allow me, I would like to see your paintings again.'

'See what you like,' William said, brusquely. 'My wife will show you where they are.'

He was obviously going to say no more so Sophy took Butts into the work-room. Ben followed them, and slid into a corner. Butts stooped over William's work and began to go through the pictures, patiently and methodically. He clearly did not want to talk so Sophy left the room. After a moment or so, dishes clattered in the kitchen and Sophy began to sing:

> 'Early one morning, just as the sun was rising,
> I heard a maiden singing in the valley below.'

Ben listened to the gentle, flowing melody:

> 'Oh don't deceive me, Oh, never leave me,
> How could you use a poor maiden so.'

Soft as it was, the song filled the house, stealing into every room, driving out the lingering gloom of the morning. Only half-thinking of what he was doing, Ben picked up a brush and set to work. The cat padded into the room and twined itself around his legs. Ben rubbed his toe along its back. And he, too, began singing.

And then Butts walked from the room and into the parlour. William was still by the fire and Butts held out the prints.

'Mr. Blake, these, these, who has seen them?'

William barely glanced at them. 'No one who has ever understood them,' he said.

'Forgive me.' Butts shook his head. 'I thought that you had friends who are artists — Mr. Fuseli, Mr. Flaxman.'

'Aye?' William's face was a mask of indifference. But the dusk was drawing in and the firelight flickered over William's face, giving it a curious vivacity, as though a spirit was playing there. 'Aye,' he repeated. 'I tell you, Mr. Butts, I am beginning to sail now on seas of my own choosing, and I leave my friends waving farewell on the quay. Let me tell you now, if you were at Godwin's because you share his views then there is no point in your being here, and there is no point in looking at my paintings.'

'I went to Godwin's to learn,' Butts said. 'And I came here for the same reason.'

'And have you learned anything?'

'I have learned that I am ignorant.'

For the first time William moved. He looked at Butts carefully. 'Those are the words of one already wise.'

'No,' Butts protested. 'I am ignorant, I know nothing. That is why I want to study your work.'

William rose and stood over Butts. His voice was grave. 'That may be dangerous.'

Butts was impatient. 'Do you think that I am afraid of the Government?'

'No. I do not think that.' William pointed to the prints. 'But what is in there might be dangerous to you. Learn the truth of what they say and you may find yourself a changed man. No longer Mr. Butts, no longer counting the country's money, no longer humdrum, but talking to angels instead of men.'

'Mr. Blake,' Butts spoke in a low voice, 'perhaps I wish to change. Has that not occurred to you?'

William's eyes widened. 'Then I say no more. Take the work, Mr. Butts.'

'Very well.' Butts gathered the prints together and turned to say farewell, but William was back in his chair, peering into the flames of the fire.

'The lad will walk you to the bridge,' he said. 'I am working.'

If Butts was surprised at this statement, coming as it did from a man who had hardly moved for two hours, he did not show it. He said good-bye and went into the kitchen.

'Good-bye, Ma'am,' he said to Sophy. 'It has been my pleasure to meet you again.'

'And mine to meet you, Sir,' Sophy answered. 'You must come again, you are welcome to share what we have.'

Ben walked with Butts to the bridge and there made his farewell. As Butts walked away, Ben called after him:

'Hey, mister. Those pictures. You ought to pay for them. Sophy's got no money.'

Without turning, Butts raised his arm, acknowledging the

call, although, dashing Ben's hopes, he did not rush back scattering guineas.

Ben shrugged and leaned over the bridge. The tide had turned. Already the river was creeping up its muddy banks, rocking the boats moored along them, scouring away the filth and rubbish which oozed from the city, cleansing, purifying, healing.

Chapter 17

Butts lived in a large comfortable house in Fitzroy Square. When he got home he took out William's work and began studying it. He was still at his desk, absorbed by the pictures, when the Watchman went past his door, calling midnight.

The next morning he went to his office in the Horse Guards where he signed receipts for the pay of the Royal Artillery, two years in arrears. He dealt with one or two routine matters then nodded to his clerks and left the building, his day's work completed.

He walked along Piccadilly, then North, through the tailors' quarter, until he came to Oxford Street. There he came upon a quiet yard which opened on to an old stable. The stable was no longer used for horses. The stalls and mangers had been knocked away and a huge window set in the roof. Around the walls were dozens of figures carved in stone and marble, nearly all of them large, and most of them muscular. Under the window was a huge block of stone. Flaxman was stooping by it, his head cocked. He was tapping the stone with a hammer and listening carefully to the sound.

Butts walked into the studio. White dust floated in the air and made him cough. At the noise Flaxman looked up.

'Yes?' he asked sharply. 'What do you want?'

'Mr. Flaxman?' Butts walked forward and introduced himself. 'That is a mighty block of stone, Sir.'

'Yes.' Flaxman cast his eye over the stone. 'It is for a statue of Hercules. It will go to Edinburgh when it is carved.'

'Edinburgh!' Butts whistled. 'I would not care to have to move it.'

'Oh, we have ways of doing that,' Flaxman said. 'I am more concerned that there might be a flaw in the stone. It doesn't ring quite true.' He tapped the block again. 'Do you hear?'

'It needs a musician's ear for that, I should think,' Butts said. 'And strong nerves to start cutting it.'

97

Flaxman agreed. 'It doesn't pay to be nervy if you are a sculptor. Well, have you come for any special purpose, Sir? Would you like to buy a Hercules of ten tons weight? It might give your doorway distinction.'

Butts smiled. 'No, Sir. I have a gargoyle there already. It looks a little too like me for comfort but I do not have the heart to knock it down. No. I have come on another matter. I want to speak about a man we both know. William Blake.'

Some of the good humour faded from Flaxman's face. 'Oh? And what is your interest in him?'

'I have his welfare at heart,' Butts said, simply.

'Have you now?' Flaxman considered for a moment, then gestured around the studio. 'You see my work, Mr. Butts.' It was not a question.

Butts needed no more prompting. 'Mine is with the Government. I am paymaster to the Army. It is not a job to make me popular in some circles, but that is what it is.'

'I have never heard of you.' Flaxman was blunt.

'No. I came prepared for that.' Butts put his hand in his pocket. 'I have a letter from Mr. Godwin.'

He pulled out a letter but Flaxman waved it aside. 'Is it not disgusting that men should have to go about mistrusting one another?'

'Yes, and that brings me back to Blake. Mrs. Blake tells me that you say he is being spied on.'

Flaxman hesitated. 'That is a little too strong, perhaps. But for sure there is something going on there.' Flaxman explained what had happened at the Royal Academy. Butts listened carefully and when Flaxman had finished he nodded.

'Braxton, you say. I know the name if not the man.'

'He is a rich man,' Flaxman said. 'Rich and powerful. He owns two hundred thousand acres and half London. He is my landlord.'

'Really?' Butts raised his eyebrows. 'Life has its ironies.'

'It irks me paying rent to a man doing such a job,' Flaxman said.

'It is a dirty job, all right. But all societies have such work done. The French have their spies, too, you know.'

Flaxman did not seem too happy at this line of argument and Butts faced him squarely.

'I have to tell you that I am not a Radical, Mr. Flaxman. I am not for changing the society in which I live by a revolution. I think that changes need to be made, but my motto is "more haste less speed".'

'Then why are you interested in Blake?' Flaxman asked.

Butts thought for a while. When he spoke his voice was deeply serious. 'Just now, you said that we cannot trust our fellow men. You may think that is the fault of the Government. I think it is because we cannot trust ourselves, and it seems to me that the reason for that is because we do not understand what is happening inside our hearts. We are profoundly ignorant of the one thing which we should know about — I mean our innermost appetites. I think that Blake is the man to teach us that. He is like a miner in the soul.' Butts suddenly smiled. 'I do not often use figures of speech.'

Flaxman had listened carefully to Butts. 'Very well,' he said. 'What do you propose, and what can I do?'

'Well, Mr. Flaxman, I don't own two hundred-thousand of anything, but I am not without some power, and you are a reputable artist of known moderation. I think that between us we might have a word with my Lord Braxton.'

'Do you think that will be effective?' Flaxman asked.

'I think it might. Commerce and Art, it can make a formidable combination.'

Flaxman was not optimistic, and said so. 'Tom Paine had friends, too, but he had to fly the country. This Braxton — I tell you, Mr. Butts, underneath the manners and the culture there is ruthlessness.'

Butts pursed his lips. 'I do not doubt it. But let us not exaggerate the matter. Blake is only a struggling artist and I think that we can make Braxton see that he is no danger to the State. At any rate, you will join me in trying?'

'Yes, I will do that,' Flaxman said. 'The question is, where and when? He goes to the Academy but there is no telling when. He may not appear there for months.'

'I have thought of that,' Butts said. 'You are a member of White's Club, are you not?'

Flaxman blinked. 'You are a knowledgeable man. Yes, I am.'

Butts smiled. 'A man I know told me. A respectable man. But what is more to the point, Braxton is a member, too. And he goes gaming there every Friday night.' He paused and looked casually at the ceiling. 'Today is Friday.'

'My word,' Flaxman said. 'I thought that you were slow but sure.'

'Yes, well,' Butts was slightly embarrassed, 'you see what

happens by speaking rashly. 'Still, if you would care to dine with me tonight we could go to White's afterwards.'

'And beard the lion in his den?'

'Or make him lie down with the lamb. Until tonight.' Butts briefly raised his hand in salute and turned away. At the door he halted and placed something down on a bench. 'My card,' he said, and then was gone.

Chapter 18

Twenty people dined with Lord Braxton that night. They sat at a long mahogany table which sparkled with silver and porcelain, and there was a servant to every guest. Braxton, splendid in purple and gold, would have been surprised to hear his dinner called sumptuous. In his eyes it was a modest affair, given by a sense of duty. The food was ordinary and the guests dull, most of them family connections, dim cousins and rural aunts, or minor political acquaintances. Bored by the company, and not, in any case, being a glutton, Braxton by-passed five of the courses and drank no more than a bottle of claret and half a bottle of port.

When the dinner was over, none of the guests lingered. Thankful that they had been noticed, or remembered, they crept off to the obscurity of their lives, leaving Braxton to his own pleasures.

At nine o'clock, the butler announced that the carriage was waiting on his Lordship's wishes. Flanked by his footmen, Braxton descended his front-door steps and, secure behind the glistening panels of his coach, was driven into the London night.

A mist hung in the air and through it the oil-lamps of Piccadilly shimmered, each lamp carrying a sparkling rainbow around it. Under the lamps faces loomed by the carriage window. In the wavering light the faces looked diseased, white and staring, like apparitions from a nightmare. And for Braxton, leaning against his morocco cushions, insulated by his gleaming coach against the night, and the people, the shuffling multitude was as insubstantial, and as irrelevant, as a dream.

In St. James's Street the carriage stopped. Braxton got out and, passing a blind beggar who could see, and a crippled beggar who could walk, he stepped into White's Club.

The foyer was blue, with elegant white mouldings of fruit and flowers swathed along the walls. Four enormous servants strode forward to meet Braxton. One took his cloak, another his hat, a third his cane, while the fourth, for want of anything else to do, bowed deeply. The servants retreated, revealing a small round man who smiled at Braxton over a double chin.

'Your Lordship is a little early tonight. Anxious to destroy your opponents, no doubt.'

'Mackrett,' Braxton acknowledged the man's presence, 'are there many in?'

'One or two, my Lord.' Mackrett spread podgy fingers.

'Lord Clearton, Mr. Cheshim, the Earl of Sunderland. I think that your Lordship will find himself accommodated.'

'I am sure I will,' Braxton murmured. 'We must not deprive you of your percentage.'

Mackrett gave a practised, meaningless chuckle: 'Running costs, my Lord, overheads. . .' and discreetly dropped away as Braxton walked into the gaming-room.

The room was large and hushed, as quiet as a church. From the tables along the walls, as from so many side chapels, quiet practised voices chanted the calls of the games: 'With you, my Lord, for five hundreds; with you, your Grace, for six hundreds; with you, Mr. Pym, for seven hundreds. . .'

As impassive as a priest, Braxton strolled along the room. Here and there men smiled at him obsequiously, and, here and there, Braxton smiled at others with the same deference. Braxton had a deep and genuine devotion to order and rank, and as it pleased him that he should be above others, so he felt no anger that others should be above him.

By a huge, open fire, a servant prowled up to him with a tray of drinks. Braxton took one and drank, lifting the glass like a salute to the room. And as he did so a quiet voice spoke from behind him: 'Lord Braxton.'

Braxton turned. Sitting by the fire, hidden from the room by a large divan, were Flaxman and Butts.

Braxton forgot neither names nor faces. 'Mr. Flaxman.' He gave a stiff bow. 'Are you a gambler?'

'No.' Flaxman stood up. 'But some of my clients are. Pray allow me to introduce Mr. Butts.'

In his turn Butts stood up and offered a bow. Braxton felt a slight flicker of distaste as he looked at the two men. They were dressed plainly, in brown and blue coats and breeches, and white stocks. They were like two Quakers, Braxton thought, and his distaste turned to irritation. The drab clothes were like a challenge, an affront to his purple and gold. What were two such dull fellows doing in his club?

'Butts,' he said. 'The name is familiar.'

'I rejoice in the title of Muster-Master General, my Lord,' Butts said. 'You may have seen my name on the Army Estimates.'

Braxton peered sharply at Butts. 'And what has the Muster-Master General come to White's for?'

'To meet you, my Lord.'

'Have you now?'

'Yes. Pray join us for a moment.' Without waiting for an answer, Butts beckoned the waiter and sat down. Flaxman joined him. Braxton sat, too, reluctantly. Inwardly he was damning Butts' impertinence, but he could hardly walk away, nor could he very well remain standing.

The play at the tables had livened now, and voices were being raised. 'Four thousand,' a man cried, hot with temper

103

and wine — 'damn it, make it five thousand.'

Braxton tilted his head. 'The stakes are becoming interesting. I have seen fifty thousand staked on a turn of a card. Guineas, that is.'

'So I have heard,' Butts said. 'But large figures do not impress me. My job, I suppose.'

Once again Braxton felt a spasm of irritation. Was the wretched clerk mocking him? He put his glass down and said sharply, 'Well, what did you want to meet me for?'

Butts smiled. 'I understand you are a collector of art, my Lord.'

'Yes.' Braxton could hardly say no, but he had a sudden uneasy feeling that in Butts' asking the question, and in he, himself, answering it, some advantage had been gained by the sober men facing him. 'Are you one?'

Butts drank, keeping Braxton waiting for an answer. When he had finished, he put down his glass and wiped his lips. 'Not as a rule. It might be, though, that we are about to become rivals.'

'Are we now?' Braxton suddenly felt more at ease. He leaned back and stretched his long legs. 'Not deadly rivals, I hope.'

Butts smiled his frank, equable smile. 'I shouldn't think so. I am too moderate a man to let matters reach such a pass. That is my conceit, anyway.'

'And mine, too,' Braxton said. 'What did the Greeks say — "all things in moderation, and moderation in all things"?'

Behind him, at one of the tables, someone shouted angrily, 'Match me five thousand,' and a sharp voice cried, 'Doubled.' Apparently indifferent to the irony, Braxton stroked his smooth cheek. 'But about what are we to become rivals, Mr. Butts?'

'Ah.' Butts folded his arms in a business-like gesture. 'Mr. Flaxman tells me that you have been asking about a man called William Blake.'

Not a flicker crossed Braxton's face. 'I mentioned him at the Academy. What is your interest in the man?'

'With respect, my Lord, I was about to ask you that question.'

The deferential phrase removed any possible insolence from the question, but again Braxton found himself in the position of being examined. This time the irritation slipped into his voice. 'He was described to me as an eccentric. Do you collect eccentrics?'

'No, No,' Butts said, good-humouredly. 'But Blake does interest me and I think him worth supporting. So does Flaxman here, and Mr. Fuseli — you will know of him, my Lord, he is an important figure at the Academy. My opinion about his art matters little, but I think that I am a judge of a man, and I think Blake worthy of support.'

'So you are going to patronize him?'

'I prefer the old term, my Lord. What was it? Take him under my protection.'

Braxton tapped his knee. 'You thought that I might decide to buy his work, is that what you meant by rivalry?'

'That is so, my Lord.'

'Then set your mind at rest. I shall not be buying. I already make a donation to the lunatics' hospital.'

'I am glad to hear both things, my Lord. I have no wish to collide with you. You have cleared my mind, and Mr. Flaxman's too, no doubt.'

The three men stood up. Braxton was a tall man and used to looking down on other men. He found that it made them uncomfortable, but Flaxman and Butts seemed unperturbed, as if they were the correct height for men to be and Braxton was somehow wrong in being tall. Braxton had an uncanny feeling that power was leaking from him to the sober men on the other side of the fire. He hesitated, seeking a way to reassert his superiority, but while he waited, Butts acted. He waved to the table.

'We mustn't keep your Lordship from your pleasures any longer. Good-night, my Lord.'

It was uncommonly like a dismissal and Braxton had no alternative but to take it. He stalked away, leaving Flaxman and Butts standing four-square before the fire like victorious generals.

After a while, and in their own time, Butts and Flaxman left the Club and began to walk home. More out of kindness than need, Butts hired a link-boy to light them home.

'Do you think that Braxton understood what we were after?' Flaxman asked.

'I think so,' Butts answered. 'I think that he will tread carefully. He knows now that Blake has friends, and not negligible ones. I will drop a word or two in Whitehall, as well.'

Flaxman gave a dry chuckle. 'You seem to know how to

deal with these matters. Braxton was off balance on his own ground.'

'Yes.' They had reached the end of Dover Street and Butts stopped, coughing as the mist caught his throat. 'Today I managed to get the Royal Artillery paid. When you know how to do that you have learned something about human nature. Besides, you know, Braxton is no fool. He will not behave like an autocrat with men like you and me watching him.'

He paused and yawned. 'It is past my bedtime. Do you want the link-boy? No? Well, here lad.' He gave the boy a coin. 'That should enable you to get a bed. Off you go.'

The boy grabbed the coin and ran off, light-footed, his torch dancing and flickering in the darkness.

'There is a Blakean image,' Flaxman said. 'Well, good-night, Butts. If you need me again you know where to find me.'

'Yes, chipping at Hercules. Good-night, Flaxman. My house is open to you. Good-night.'

An hour later both men were in bed, Butts placid between white sheets, Flaxman in his, dreaming of his Hercules. In Levant Court Grale slept too, sweating underneath a dirty blanket, moaning and snorting, but asleep, unconscious, in a merciful oblivion. But Braxton was awake, flipping over the cards with long white fingers, matching his guineas in hundreds and thousands, and losing steadily.

And in Hercules Buildings William was also awake. He sat before the fire, motionless, hour after hour. The fire burned down and thin flames, pale blue and green, raised their evil heads from the charred timber like snakes.

'These flames are not purifying,' William said. 'They come from disease and rot, Robert.' And Robert, sitting across the fire, leaned forward, nodding eagerly, the blue and green light wavering across his white cheeks.

'The world is sick, Robert,' William said, and 'Yes, yes,' Robert whispered.

'I have written a song,' William said. Robert whispered, 'Read it to me.' And William read his new song:

'O Rose, thou art sick!
The invisible worm,
That flies in the night,
In the howling storm.

Has found out thy bed
Of crimson joy;
And his dark secret love
Does thy life destroy.'

Chapter 19

Lord Braxton spent the week-end on his estate in Buckinghamshire. He was extremely unpleasant to his servants, and a tenant farmer found himself no longer a tenant of Lord Braxton. But when he returned to Town on Monday he had regained his habitual air of ironical detachment. Ferril, calling in the afternoon to make his weekly report, found him as urbane and quizzical as ever. He listened patiently as Ferril plodded through his report and signed the accounts.

'That is all?' he asked.

Ferril gathered his papers. 'Almost, my Lord. There is just one more thing.'

'There is always is, Mr. Ferril. Well?'

'About the man, Blake. The poem, the one about the Revolution.'

'Ah yes.' Braxton opened his drawer and took out the manuscript. 'It is of no interest to us. See it is returned, if you can.'

'Very well, my Lord.' Ferril was regretful but resigned. 'There is no code then?'

'No.' Braxton paced across to the window. A fog was forming. Dirty yellow trails of vapour hung among the spires of Westminster. Braxton tapped the window restlessly.

'Have you ever been to Italy, Mr. Ferril?'

Ferril admitted that he never had.

'It is a beautiful country, beautiful. Blue skies, sunshine. It makes one wonder why one lives in this gloomy island.'

Ferril, who had no doubts about why he did, made vague clucking noises which could have been sympathetic. 'Should I keep a man on Blake, my Lord?' he asked.

Braxton did not answer for a while. He stood, tapping on the window, looking out on the rolling fog. His breath blurred the glass and he rubbed it impatiently, as if there was something outside he wished to see.

'I was warned off Blake last Friday night, Mr. Ferril,' he said. 'Two dowdy men called at my Club and told me —

suggested — that I should not take any steps to harass him.'

'My Lord!' Ferril tried to show a virtuous and shocked indignation, but he was as snuffingly curious as a dog at a rat-hole.

'It would appear that this Blake has friends, Ferril.'

'I see, my Lord.' Ferril nodded wisely. 'Would these be important friends, Sir?'

Braxton hesitated. 'The answer to that penetrating question is yes, and no. They are... new men, Ferril, middling men. On their own they are of no account but there are many of them. They are as persistent as ants, creeping everywhere, in the City, in Parliament; and they are careful, careful men, Ferril.' Centuries of disdain crept into Braxton's voice as he said the words. As he spoke, a vision of Italian skies swept across Braxton's mind and he felt a longing to escape from the dark room, and the dark city, to a land where there were no careful men.

'Butts,' he whispered, half to himself. 'Butts and Flaxman, what names!'

'Should I mark them down, Sir?' asked Ferril.

'What? Yes, mark them down. But no action is to be taken against them without my written order.'

'Very good, my Lord.' Ferril scratched at his paper. 'And I am to take my man off Blake?'

'Yes.'

'Just as you say, my Lord. He is not dangerous then?'

'What? Oh yes, he is dangerous. He has a knack of making men think, and that is always dangerous. If I had my own way I would hang him as high as Haman.'

'Yes, well, of course, if your Lordship has been warned...' Disapproval seeped from Ferril like gas from a sewer.

'Oh, it is not that.' Braxton left the window and walked to his desk. 'But Blake — I made one or two inquiries of my own. The booksellers do not stock his books, his prints are not sold, and now he is to have a patron. He has no voice, Ferril. The mob will never hear him and his patron will draw his fangs.'

'But I thought that your Lordship said — ' Ferril began, but Braxton cut him short.

'That he was dangerous, yes. But he is a menace because he makes some men look inside themselves, doubting and questioning. He is like a spot of mildew, spreading and corrupting, but slowly. He is not a man who will bother us in our generation, but when I think of the future. . . well, leave it for now. We have other fish to fry.'

For an hour or so after that they sat together, heads bent in the darkened room, as they prepared their fish for the frying.

As Braxton and Ferril talked in Whitehall, away in the East of the city, in his reeking room, Hector Grale was getting ready to go out. No preparations could have been simpler. He rose from his bed where he had snored the afternoon away, put on his hat, and walked out. He was going to call on William Blake.

In Newgate Street there was a heavy mist, but not enough to stop the traffic. Drays and wagons clashed deafeningly on the cobbles and the endless, ceaseless crowd jostled along, cursing and swearing, as mindless in their march as lemmings.

Grale staggered along with the mob, his head splitting with the noise, but as he drew near St. Paul's, its dome lost in the mist, the streets became quiet, hushed. The savage pains in his head eased and left only a dull ache. As he shambled through Fleet Street he was oddly mixed in his emotions. He longed for the warmth and stillness of William's house, and Sophy's gentleness, and that both would be offered he had no doubt. But always the thought of Ferril's guineas floated before his eyes. He tried to push the thought away. 'Blake is a traitor,' he muttered. 'I am a patriot. I am guarding my country. My country,' he said, desperately, as the filth of the streets soaked through his broken shoes and the fog froze on the back of his neck.

By the time he had reached the Strand full night had fallen and the fog was dense, rolling off the river and oozing from the narrow lanes which led down to the water. He groped his way forward and found himself in an alley. He slipped on the cobbles and fell heavily. He dragged himself to his feet and limped back the way he had come but turned down another lane, and into another. He was in a labyrinth of alleyways, closed and shuttered, and silent in the fog.

Wheezing and shivering he lurched along, and then found himself ankle-deep in slime, and realized that he had come to the river's edge. He stood, exhausted, listening to the oily slop of the river, and, straining his eyes, peered into the curtain of fog before him. 'Lost myself,' he said, and felt the bitter taste of fog on his lips. Then something soft flopped in the slime and scrabbled over his shoes. He gave a cry of terror and started back, falling again. He scrambled up the cobbles and found a wall and followed it round a corner, back to the Thames. For a time he leaned against the wall, almost asleep. Out on the river a bell jangled and a man's hoarse cry of alarm answered it as some reckless boatman took his craft

downstream. Grale wanted to shout, too. He wanted to cry, 'There is a man here. Hector Grale is here.' Instead his mouth cracked into a rictus and he dragged himself away.

Eventually he found himself back on a street, among people, but farther from Hercules Buildings than when he had started. He limped east while behind him the fog loomed, impenetrable, over the river.

At first his intention was to go to Levant Court, but as he neared Gray's Inn he found himself moving, as if being pulled by an invisible rope, down to the Old Bailey, to Ferril's cellar.

And Ferril was there, his face with its dog-like snout sticking from his gingery whiskers.

'Well,' he snapped. 'What do you want?'

Grale dragged his arm across his face. 'Evening, Sir. Number 37.' Ferril's face seemed to be wavering, rippling, like a reflection in water. Grale put his hands on the desk in an effort to steady himself. 'I've been to see that William Blake. You remember, Sir, William Blake.'

'Have you now?' Ferril gave his animal laugh. 'How did you get there, swim?'

'Swim?' Grale was bewildered by the question, and then he looked down at himself. He was plastered with mud. 'Oh,

111

fell. Fell in the fog, Sir. But I've got some news for you.'

'London Bridge fallen down?' Ferril snickered again, hugely delighted with his wit.

'Oh no, no.' Grale flapped his arm feebly. 'No, it's. . .' It's what? he thought, and groped in the depths of his soul for a lie. But there was none there.

'I'll come tomorrow,' he said. 'First thing; tell you then, yes.'

'Don't bother.' Ferril had his ledger open. 'We're not interested in Blake any more. 37 aren't you? Yes, well — ' He struck a line through Grale's name, noting the guinea payment with regret. 'Don't come again, 37. You're off the pay-roll.'

'Off?' Grale couldn't believe what he had heard. 'Mr. Ferril, it's not right.'

Ferril cackled again. 'Ha, ha, ha. Hee hee hee. Not right! Dear me, you're almost worth the money for a laugh. He rocked in his chair. 'Ha ha ha. Here.' He pushed *The French Revolution* across the desk. 'Get that back to Blake. And see that you don't talk. You understand that? One word from you and I'll have you chained in Bedlam for the rest of your natural — got that?'

Dimly Grale got it. 'Yes, Sir. I'll get some information for you about someone else.'

Ferril leaned forward, hissing, 'I've just told you — never come back here again. Now, out.'

'All right, Sir,' Grale said, too exhausted even to beg. He walked to Newgate Street, stupified by fatigue. 'I'm a bag of rubbish,' he whispered. 'That's all I am, a bag of rubbish walking about.'

At Levant Court he dragged himself up the stairs, went into his room, and fell on to the bed. He lay there until his legs stopped quivering, then, half-falling from the bed, he crawled across the room and drank some water from a dish. 'Rubbish,' he said. 'Rubbish.'

Somehow he got back to his bed and dragged his blanket over himself. His leg began twitching again and he was tormented with itching. From the rooms about his came screams, bangs, animal whoops, as the inhabitants of Levant Court arrived home. But exhaustion claimed Grale in the end and he slept. And in his sleep the years slipped from his face. Wrapped in his blanket he looked strangely like the child in its cocoon which William had drawn, and, in his sleep, like ᵗhat infant, he, too, dreamed of immortality.

Chapter 20

The morning after Grale was lost in the fog, William, Sophy, and Ben sat around their table having breakfast. When they had finished, William went into the work-room with Ben.

'Do you like engraving, Ben?' William asked.

Ben thought that he did, and said so.

William said no more but put on his coat. Ben asked him where he was going.

'To find work. Someone might have a daub they need engraving. Would you care to come and see what it is like to be a beggar?'

Ben was irritated by the expression. The spark of rebellion he had felt the week before, when William had been indifferent to Sophy's tears, suddenly licked up into a flame.

'There's nothing wrong in asking for work,' he said. 'Everyone has to do it. It's not begging.'

'You think not?' William was ironical. 'Let me tell you, Ben, I will get some work today. Old acquaintances will find some scraps to cut, and they will pay me for them. Then they will throw them into the bin and some journeyman's work will be used instead. That seems like begging to me.'

'But why will they throw them away?' Ben insisted.

'Do you not know yet?'

Ben shrugged. He did know. William would engrave as he wished, not as the customer wanted. It was pointless arguing.

'Do you want to come with me?' William asked teasingly.

'All right.' Ben put his coat on, and the tails no longer needed pinning up.

But as they prepared to go out, there was a knock on the front door. A minute later Sophy called to William that there was someone to see him. They went into the parlour and found two bulky men standing before the fire.

'Mr. Blake?' one asked.

William admitted that he was and the man held out an envelope.

'Mr. Butts sent this for you. If you would sign this receipt, please.'

William signed and the two men left, refusing Sophy's offer of a glass of milk.

William placed the envelope on the table, unopened. Sophy was openly curious, and Ben, excited and impatient.

'Aren't you going to open it?' he demanded.

'Yes.' William had the manner of a man about to shoulder a grievous burden. 'Yes, we will open it, but I fear what is in there, Ben. I fear it. Sophy — ' He nodded at the table.

Sophy took a knife and picked up the envelope. 'It is heavy,' she said.

'That it is,' William agreed. 'And no heavier weight ever came into this house. Open it.'

Sophy slit the envelope. A handful of guineas clattered on to the table. Sophy and Ben stared at the coins, amazed. 'Crikey,' Ben gasped. 'It's money!'

Sophy's face flushed scarlet. She held out her hand and touched the coins nervously, as if she was afraid her touch would make them disappear.

'Guineas,' she whispered. 'One, two, three, goodness me! Ten — fifteen guineas, William, fifteen guineas!'

She clapped her hands together and Ben gave a piercing whistle, but William spoke sharply.

'What else is in there?'

Sophy looked into the envelope and fished out a sheet of notepaper, her face alight with happiness.

'Read it,' William said.

Sophy held the letter to the light and read:

'Dear Mr. Blake,

'When I left your house last week you allowed me to take some of your work with me. I am assuming that this is for sale and I wish to buy it. I enclose fifteen guineas as an earnest of my intentions. I am engaged for the next few days and shall be out of Town. But when I return I hope you will permit me to call on you and discuss the full charge you wish to make. May I say that I am anxious to buy as much of your work as you are prepared to sell.

'I have had a few words with Lord Braxton since I saw you last.

'Your obedient servant,
  'Thomas Butts.'

'Fifteen guineas!' Ben was still staggered.

114

'Yes, and more to come,' Sophy cried. 'Oh William, some-one knows your worth.'

'Aye.' There was no pleasure in William's voice. 'It has come to this,' he muttered.

Ben missed the chill in William's voice, but Sophy didn't. 'But William,' she said, 'Mr. Butts is going to buy your work, and he has seen that Lord Braxton, too. Just think, now you won't have to go tramping for work. This money will keep us for weeks, and all because of Mr. Butts!'

'Yes. All because of Mr. Butts.' William was bitter. 'Not because the world has seen what I have seen, or heard what I have heard; not because we live in a land where honest men are safe, but because of Mr. Butts.'

Ben had stopped staring at the money and caught up with the conversation. 'Aren't you glad?' he asked, hardly able to believe his ears.

'Let it be,' William said. 'Let it be.' He leaned across the table and picked up some of the money. 'I am going out. I will be back in two or three hours. Take what is there, Sophy. It was given with a good heart I have no doubt.'

He walked to the door and halted. 'Come with me, Ben. You will see something more interesting than guineas.'

Ben frowned. He wanted to stay with Sophy and count the money again — and again — but there was something in William's voice which suggested that there was to be no argument. He stole a glance at Sophy. She tilted her chin fractionally, and Ben went.

They crossed the familiar bridge and plunged into the din of the city.

'Where are we going?' Ben asked.

'To look at Hell,' William answered, and Ben asked no more.

An hour's tramp brought them to a roaring highway, choked with flocks of sheep being driven into the markets. After a mile or so William turned suddenly into a filthy doorway and up a flight of rotting stairs. At the top of the stairs William halted before a door.

'Now,' he said to Ben, 'meet your enemy,' and hammered on the door.

There was no answer and William struck the door again. 'Mr. Grale,' he shouted.

In the room something moved, dragging itself across the floor. There was an odd, scratching noise behind the door, the knob turned, and Hector Grale stood in the doorway.

'I hope that we haven't disturbed you,' William said.

Grale gave a ghastly smile. 'No,' he whispered. 'No. I am glad that you have called. Come in, come.'

He lurched backwards and banged into his box. 'Excuse me. I am not too well. No, not too well.' He shook his head as if baffled by his weakness. 'Pray sit down.' He gestured to the box and himself fell on the bed. 'You will have to stand, lad,' he said to Ben.

'That's all right,' Ben muttered. He stood by the window, looking down on Grale. The man looked sick and old: much older and much sicker than Ben remembered. And he was dirty, dirtier than even Ben himself had been when William had found him, and it seemed to Ben somehow more disgusting that an old man should be dirty. Ben felt a wave of moral superiority and revulsion as he stood by the window in his russet suit and stout green coat. He scowled at Grale, who saw the expression.

'Your boy doesn't like me, Mr. Blake,' he said, and grinned mirthlessly.

'No, he doesn't,' William said.

Grale gave a despairing laugh. 'Young men, they are ready to judge.' He leaned back against the greasy wall as if the effort of speaking had exhausted him.

'Yes, they are willing to sit in the seat of Moses,' William agreed. He appeared unsurprised and undisturbed by Grale's filth. 'Did you take a poem from my house, Mr. Grale?'

A nerve began to twitch and flicker on Grale's cheek. 'A poem? I. . . I. . .'

'I think you did,' William said. 'The lad here saw you.'

'Yes.' Grale licked his lips. 'Yes, I remember now. I did take it. I wanted to read it. I am sorry.'

'I would like it back, if you have finished with it,' William said, politely.

Grale's jowls trembled with eagerness. 'I have it,' he cried. He heaved himself from the bed and hobbled across the room to a bundle in the corner and fumbled for a moment. 'Here, Mr. Blake. You see, I have it safe.'

'Thank you.' William took the poem and put it in his pocket without looking at it.

'I should not have taken it,' Grale said. 'But you were not there to ask.'

'That is quite all right. I am glad you took it.' William

leaned forward and touched Grale's knee. 'How are you, Mr. Grale? You look unwell.'

'Yes, I am not well. I must admit that. I caught a chill last night. I was out. . .'

'In that fog?'

'Yes, in the fog. I fell down, in the mud. I was coming to see you, Mr. Blake. But I had to turn back.'

'You would have been welcome.' William looked at the bundle in the corner. 'Are you packing your belongings?'

Grale nodded hopelessly. 'The agent has told me to go. He told me this morning. I haven't paid the rent.'

Ben felt a wicked surge of pleasure at Grale's remark, and admired William's calm questioning. It was better than hitting Grale. Slower, but better.

'Where are you going to live?' William asked.

Grale shook his head. His cheek was flickering violently and a little flake of dirt fell from his face. No one spoke for a while, but the room was not silent. From the road came the din of the noonday traffic and the bleating of sheep. Finally William stirred.

'I came here to give you money, Mr. Grale. Two paltry guineas. What shoddiness. It is disgraceful.' He shook his head. 'Disgraceful. I think you had better come back to Lambeth with us.'

Grale looked at William in disbelief. 'Go with you?' he repeated. 'To Lambeth?'

'That is so.'

'And stay with you, and Mrs. Blake?'

'I don't think that Mrs. Blake is going to leave,' William said.

Grale pawed feebly at his coat. 'I. . . I. . .' His voice died away.

William understood Grale's meaning. 'We have plenty of hot water. Anyone would get dirty who fell in the mud. . .' He stood up. 'Come, Mr. Grale.'

Grale struggled to his feet and lurched forward. William caught him by the elbow. 'I don't think that you will be able to walk all the way. Ben, go down the street and see if you can find a carriage. There must be a haulier around here.'

Ben could not believe his ears. 'Get a carriage for him,' he burst out.

'That is what I said.' William's voice was quiet but there was a steady pressure behind it and, red-faced, Ben yielded.

He slouched from the room and down the stairs, on to the street.

A few hundred yards down the highway he found a livery stable, and a scrubby, unshaven man agreed to provide a carriage. 'Round in half an hour,' he said. 'Cash in advance.'

'All right,' Ben agreed and wandered back to Levant Court. Half-way there, underneath a barber's red and white pole, a hawker was selling prints.

'Here you are,' he bellowed. 'Horrible murder in White-chapel, see the picture — Dandy Williams hanged at Tyburn, see the picture, read his dying speech — French King having his head cut off, see the picture — all coloured — see the pictures, all coloured, farthing each.'

The man bellowed on, apparently inexhaustible, shaking the wooden frame on which the prints were tacked. Ben paused and watched the man. A bricklayer walking past bought a print of the highwayman's hanging. A milkmaid bought a print of the King's death. An old woman shuffled by and bought an account of the murder. Ben himself fished out a farthing and bought a print, pointing to one at random.

As he walked back to William and Grale he looked at his purchase. A fleet of ships, each identical, and each carrying an enormous Union Flag, sailed across a poisonously blue sea. Underneath, a sailor with vaguely crossed eyes stood with arms akimbo. From his mouth floated an enormous bubble with words in it. Ben stopped and squinted at the words. 'We'll give those Frogs a drubbing. One jolly British tar is worth ten of them. Their frogs' legs will never hop over Britain's wooden walls.' Below the seaman was a poem. Ben stumbled his way through it:

> 'We are Jolly British Sailor-boys,
> Jolly lads are we,
> We will give the Frogs a drubbing,
> And drive them from the sea.
> God bless our King and country,
> And it God bless again,
> For it boys, and for FREEDOM,
> We will fight with might and main.
> We jolly British sailor-lads,
> We will defend the seas,
> To keep you safe from base revolt,
> And save your liberties!'

118

Ben could hardly decide which was worse, the drawing or the poem, but both had a crude life about them, and a direct quality, without frills, as if whoever had made the print knew exactly what he had to say, and who he was saying it to. The print had been taken from a woodcut and Ben looked at it with something of a professional eye. It reminded him of something but what he could not call to mind. It was as he was entering Levant Court that he remembered. The print had the vitality and directness of the Hogarth one William had shown him months before.

Chapter 21

Ben sat in the work-room listening to Grale coughing in the bedroom upstairs. The cough had begun the night after Grale had been carried into Hercules Building. For three days since then it had continued, a terrible racking noise that sounded as if Grale's chest was being torn apart. Hour after hour the cough went on until Ben felt as if his own lungs were choked and suffocating.

When Ben went out to escape the sound, it followed him. Leaning over the bridge, or walking in the sodden water meadows, some muffled sound would trigger off an association in his mind and for a second he would strain his ears, convinced that he could hear the cough.

A doctor came and went, taking a guinea with him; Sophy made broth and tried to feed Grale, but for the three days he lay in his spasm, it was William who stayed by his side, day and night, unmoving, sleepless.

Ben sat and half-heartedly touched in an illustration for the *Songs*, baffled by the care both William and Sophy were taking over the old man; and then something made him lift his head sharply, like a dog. The coughing had stopped and the house was as silent as a grave.

'He is dead,' he thought. 'The old man is dead!' To his amazement his eyes filled with tears. 'Why,' he whispered, 'I thought I would be glad.' It was incredible. One moment a man had been lying in the bed; a filthy, disgusting, lying creature, but a man. And now? Nothing. A hole in the universe. His hand trembled and he put down the brush he was holding. As he did so he looked again at the song.

> For Mercy has a human heart,
> Pity a human face,
> And Love, the human form divine,
> And Peace, the human dress.

A shadow fell across the page and looking up he saw William.

'Is he dead?' he asked. 'Mr. Grale?'

William bent and looked closely at Ben. 'You are crying?'

Ben brushed his arm across his eyes. 'No,' he said, defiantly.

William gave a grim smile. 'You are a creature of rebellion, Ben, at war with angels and devils alike. No, Mr. Grale is not dead. He is asleep. The fever has left him and he should be better in a few days. But suppose we had not met him, where would he be now?'

Ben did not answer and William repeated the question.

'Where, Ben?'

Again Ben was silent and William answered for him.

'He would be dead in a hole, like a poisoned rat. You do not like Mr. Grale, Ben, that is clear, and indeed there is no reason why you should. But when Jesus Christ told us to love our neighbours he said nothing about liking them. You have never read Shakespeare but I will quote him at you. "If every man was treated according to his deserts, who would escape flogging?" Who, Ben? To be sure, if I was treated according to mine I would be whipped from here to Dover.'

He paused and lifted up the *Songs*. ' "Mercy, Pity, Peace, and Love." I was a child when I wrote those words. Colour this instead.'

He laid down a piece of paper. Hesitantly Ben picked up the poem and read it:

A Divine Image

> Cruelty has a human heart,
> And Jealousy a human face;
> Terror the human form divine,
> And Secrecy the human dress.
>
> The human dress is forgèd iron,
> The human form a fiery forge,
> The human face a furnace seal'd,
> The human heart its hungry gorge.

'Both songs are true, Ben,' William said. 'From the war of contraries the truth arises. And you have cried, and your tears were those of a man and not a child, for you cried for the suffering of the world and not your own. Those tears will

121

soften your own suffering, Ben. Be sure of that.'

My suffering, Ben wondered, and felt a tremor of fear. What suffering could he undergo? He was not an old man like Grale.

William straightened himself and stretched his arms.

'I am going to walk for a while. Come with me, Ben.'

Ben got his coat and the two of them walked as far as the bridge. Half-way along it William halted. Automatically Ben leaned over the parapet to see what was happening on the river. Dozens of barges were butting their way downstream and wherries and ferry-boats were dodging about them, the oarsmen bawling abuse and threats as the larger craft bore down on them. The air was cold, biting, and for all its dullness the day had a human zest to it which Ben liked.

'Do you remember the first day we came here?' William said.

'Yes, we were going to the New Church. We met Mr. Grale that day, and the man from the oil shop shouted at us.' The memory came back to him as though he were seeing a picture. Himself, scrawny, frightened, in tattered breeches and a coat two sizes too large for him. With a shock he realized that it had been only a few months ago. 'It seems a long time since,' he said.

'Oh yes,' William said. 'But time is not doled out in equal rations, like a soldier's dinner. An hour can hold all of Eternity. Change leaps on us, Ben, and when it leaves us we are utterly changed. Utterly.'

He was silent for a while. The wind, which had ruffled his red hair, died away. The voices of the boatmen came echoing flatly off the water, and from the city came a steady muted rumble. Something damp fell on Ben's hand. He looked up. Flakes of snow were drifting down from a steely sky. Across the river lights began to glow.

William turned on his elbow. 'When we were at Grale's, when you went for the carriage, you bought a broadsheet.'

'What?' Ben looked up, puzzled, then his face cleared as he remembered.

'Oh yes.'

'You liked it, I think, Ben.'

'Yes.' A thought occurred to Ben. 'How did you know?'

'I saw you through the window. . .'

'Oh.' Ben's lips rounded. How much William saw. Those blue eyes, which looked into infinity, saw the smallest movement.

122

'Do you have it on you?' William asked. 'I should like to see it, if I may.'

Ben searched through his pockets and pulled out the crumpled print. William studied it carefully, shielding it from the snow with his hand. The jaunty seaman stared back at him, his cross eyes giving him a vaguely criminal look.

'Why do you like this, Ben?' William asked.

Ben groped for the words which would explain the attraction. 'It's, it's. . .' He waved his hand and the gesture, quite unintentionally, embraced the river and the city.

'Yes,' William said. 'It has life.' He carefully folded the print and gave it back to Ben. The snow was falling thicker now, wheeling dizzily through the air. Through the flakes the river looked black, impenetrable, as sinister as the Styx. Night was coming in with the tide. Against its darkness William's face was as white as the snowflakes. It was bitterly cold, but still William did not move.

'Last week I asked you if you liked engraving, Ben. You said that you did. It is a good craft, but you will learn little from me.'

'Why not?' Ben asked. 'Aren't you going to teach me?' He was stung and hurt by William's remark.

'It is not that. I would willingly teach you all I know. But to learn a craft needs practice. What practice will you get with me? An hour or two's work a week, if we are lucky.'

Ben choked down a faint feeling of panic. 'You're going to get plenty of work,' he said. 'Mr. Butts is going to buy everything you do.'

'That is true. Mr. Butts has arrived like Father Christmas down the chimney. But his gifts are gall and wormwood to me, Ben.' William gestured to the city, glowing in the dusk behind the screen of snow. 'That is the greatest city on this earth, Ben, perhaps the greatest city that there has ever been. There are houses in it where Midas would be accounted a beggar, prisons where Torquemada would be thought a novice, temples where God Himself would not be welcome if he came in the guise of a carpenter. And I have spent forty years in this city and for twenty of them I have cried aloud in the streets, teaching the love of God and the understanding of mankind. But how many people know me? Not two dozen, and of those not ten have an inkling of what I am saying. Now comes Mr. Butts. One man.'

'One man is better than no man,' Ben said practically. 'And he's going to pay you.'

'I have said before, Ben, that you have an eye for fact. You will be at home in this world. Do I sound ungrateful to Mr. Butts? I do not mean to be, but I wished for the eyes and ears of the million, now I shall be working for one alone.

street. It was May, and spring had found its way even into London. The sun struggled through the grimy air and sparrows were busy along the house eaves. Ben cajoled a girl who was hawking flowers and salad into giving him a daffodil. He stuck it in his lapel and strolled along the street, utterly self-confident, waving to his numerous aquaintances, a London apprentice to the life.

He cut through the tangle of alleys behind Cheapside and crossed the river by London Bridge, stopping here and there at the shops along it to cast a professional eye at the prints on sale.

On the Southwark side he quickened his pace through the leafy lanes which bordered the pleasure gardens and by four o'clock he was at Hercules Buildings where he found Sophy waiting for him at the gate.

Sophy's face lit up as she saw Ben. 'You knew that I would be here,' Ben called.

'That I did,' said Sophy. 'Your dinner is on the stove.'

Arm in arm they went into the kitchen. 'Where is William?' Ben asked.

'At Mr. Butts'. He spends a deal of time there.'

Ben looked at Sophy's cheerful face. 'You look happy, these days.'

'Yes.' Contentment glowed from Sophy.

'And William, is he happy?'

The slightest shadow crossed Sophy's face. 'I think so. It is hard to tell with him. But he is working and he has met more people at Mr. Butts' who are interested in his work.' She went to the stove and looked into a pan. 'Your dinner is ready. Do you want it now?'

'Yes, thank you.' Ben lingered at the window for a moment and looked at the hedge where he had skulked the first day he had entered Hercules Buildings. What had he looked like then? More like a hedgehog than a human being. A patch of white caught his attention and he craned forward. He was looking at Grale's face as the man slept in a chair under the medlar-tree.

'How is he — Grale?' Ben asked as he turned and sat at the table.

Sophy paused as she ladled out broth. 'Oh, he is much better now. Mr. Butts is going to find him a job in Whitehall, a doorman, I think.' She watched Ben as he began to eat. 'Is it all right? I put lots of barley in it.'

'It's lovely,' Ben assured her. 'Just as I like it.'

'And you are happy, aren't you?' Sophy asked again, anxiously.

'I am. I really am.' As he spoke, Ben remembered the bitterness of that night in the winter, as the snow fell silently from the black sky, and his new-found manhood dissolved in tears. 'I never thought I would be again. Happy, I mean.'

Sophy followed his thought. 'Nor did I. I cried myself to sleep, too. I heard you sobbing and I wanted to come down the stairs but William told me not to. He said if I did I would never send you away.'

'He was right there.' Ben waved his spoon, very much the man of the world. 'I just couldn't believe it, Sophy. I was to be cast out, and Mr. Grale was to stay. The world was turned upside-down that night, all right.'

'Yes. William didn't like it either, you know. But I was firm about you going. I was worried that you might end up without a proper trade in your fingers. Ah well, it's all come right in the end.' Sophy shook her head and took away Ben's plate.

Ben started on a leg of lamb while Sophy looked on approvingly. 'Will you speak to Mr. Grale afterwards?' she asked.

Ben gave a non-committal grunt. Since he had left the Blakes' he had scarcely seen Grale. When he called on his weekly visit the old man kept out of the way, whether under orders or not Ben neither knew nor cared.

He demolished the lamb and ate a custard, stopping only to reassure Sophy that he was being well fed by Mrs. Fox, and not ill-treated by Mr. Fox. The clock ticked away and a warm breeze blew through the window, fluttering the checked curtains. It was all very agreeable and as he scraped his plate Ben decided that, if he did see Grale, he would be, if not actually affable, then at least not unpleasant.

When he had finished he helped Sophy to wash up then sauntered into the work-room. He was bending over a drawing of William's when a shadow fell over him and, looking up, he saw the man himself.

Despite himself, Ben felt, as he always did, a slight flicker of apprehension. 'Hello, William,' he said, nervously.

'Ben.' William returned the greeting. His blue eyes were as visionary as ever and his face still pale, translucent almost. 'Are you well?'

130

'Yes.' Ben's answer was a throaty whisper. He cleared his throat. 'Yes,' he said again loudly. 'Yes, thank you.'

'And how is the engraving?' William asked.

'All right, William. Mr. Fox says that I am doing well. He is going to send me to a drawing-school next month.'

'I am glad to hear it. And are you cutting curves yet?'

'Only practising, but Mr. Fox says that I can cut some on the next print.'

'Well, it's all in turning the wheel. When you can do that you will cut as well as any man alive. I always said that you had the eye for an engraver. Come into the garden. It is too nice to stay indoors.'

They brushed past the familiar vine and walked under the trees. Grale was still asleep in his chair, his face turned innocently to the sun. He looked quite different now. His face was pink, the lines which scored it, which before had expressed misery and cunning, now seemed merely the marks of a harmless old age. He opened his eyes as William and Ben approached him.

'Dozed off,' he said. 'Hello, Ben.'

'Hello, Mr. Grale,' Ben answered.

'Working hard?' Grale smiled, and even his grin was no longer the death's head rictus it had been.

'Your dinner is ready,' William said.

Grale stood up and walked flat-footedly to the house. William took the chair he had left and Ben lay on the grass. The cat jumped out of the hedge and rubbed its back against Ben's leg. Ben breathed a sigh of contentment.

'Here we are, where we began,' he said. 'Both of us in the garden.'

'Our bodies are where they were, but our spirits have changed long since. Changed utterly.' William lay back in his chair. 'Changed utterly,' he repeated.

Ben pulled a blade of grass and teased the cat with it. What William had said was true, he thought. To be sure they had changed, or, rather, he and Grale had altered. Who would ever have thought that Grale could look so harmless, or who seeing himself, Ben Pendrill, in the hedge that day last year, would have imagined him as he was today, sturdy, clean, clear-eyed. But it was William who had seen that in both of them. His visionary eyes had seen that. Ben felt a sudden burst of affection and touched William's foot.

'I have never thanked you for what you did for me,' he

said. 'But I do.'

William brushed the thanks aside. 'It was nothing. It is Sophy you should thank. You know that it was her decision that you should leave us? She saw where your true interests lay. I was as blind as a bat, and selfish with it. I would have kept you with us but she saw that you would become a dependant, like a poor relation, living on us instead of making your own life.'

Ben was anxious that William should get some credit. 'It was you who saw Mr. Fox and got me apprenticed.'

William shrugged. 'It was Sophy who thought of that. Mr. Butts paid the sixty guineas premium — I was but the messenger-boy. No, it was Sophy's doing.' He half smiled. 'I thought that she would break her heart the day you left.'

'But she was smiling,' Ben said.

'Yes. You will not often see such bravery. We have never been blessed with children.'

They sat in silence for a while. A soft wind rustled the leaves of the tree, a thrush trilled from the hedge, the cat lay on its back, yawning at the sky.

'How is your work, William?' Ben asked. 'Are the *Songs of Experience* finished?'

'Almost. I have etched most of them and Sophy has done a deal of colouring this winter. But I shall write no more of them. It is a time for change.'

'Sophy told me that you might get more work from the booksellers,' Ben said.

'Yes, that is so.' William did not sound enthusiastic. 'But that is mere labour. It will buy us bread, but my work, the fruits of my life, that is yet to come.'

For a while he was silent. The light of day was fading. A night moth, the first of the evening, fluttered from the darkness and landed on Ben's sleeve. He put out his finger and the moth crept over it. William had written a line about a moth — what was it? Ben searched his memory; yes, that was it: 'Kill not the moth nor butterfly, for the Last Judgement draweth nigh.'

Ben shivered a little. The Day of Judgement — who would stand unafraid when that time came? Suddenly the dusk seemed darker and the trees, tapping their twigs overhead, were like accusers against that day. He looked at William, a silent black figure in his chair. How was it that the man could move one so, transforming the world by the use of an image,

132

or an idea?

As if William read Ben's mind he spoke again. 'I feel great shapes about me. What they are I do not as yet know, but that they are there is beyond any doubt. My eyes shall be opened soon and I shall see, and speak. And not myself, alone. Angels and devils, ghosts, visions, the spirits which guide men's minds and form their hearts, they will not be denied for ever. The everlasting gospel will be proclaimed, and not by me alone. Be assured, there are men now living whose eyes will see and whose mouths will speak.'

Again they sat in silence and then Sophy came through the dusk with Grale.

'We thought that we would like to join you while the day lasts,' she said.

The four sat quietly in the garden. The thrush sang its last, wild song; a crow beat its way home, hardly visible in the twilight; a silver moon rose; a star shone, and another.

Sophy sighed. 'All things turn to their slumbers.'

'Work, for the night cometh, when no man shall work,' Grale said, unexpectedly, and stroked his waistcoat in a satisfied way.

'Yes,' Sophy said, and 'Yes,' said Ben, too. But as he spoke he looked at William, his face white in the moonlight, and doubted if it was true for him.

'Tell us a poem, William,' Sophy asked. 'Ben has not heard the one you wrote last.'

William shook his head, but Sophy pressed him. 'Ben lived with us through the *Songs of Experience* and he knows all but this one.'

William hesitated, then agreed. 'It is right that he should hear it. Yes, when he is a grown man and has forgotten us he may remember the song he heard an old man tell in a garden, in the darkness.'

Ben gave an indignant and hurt cry but William laid his hand on the lad's head.

'No, I jested. You will not forget us, Ben, nor we you, ever. Now hear.'

He rose from his chair, blotting out the moon. 'Hear,' he said. 'Hear me, men and ghosts, those dead and those yet to be. Aye, hear the voice of one who cries in the wilderness, hear the voice of William Blake:

'Hear the voice of the Bard!

Who present, past, and future, sees;
    Whose ears have heard
    The Holy Word
That walk'd among the ancient trees,

Calling the lapsèd soul,
And weeping in the evening dew;
    That might control
    The starry pole,
And fallen, fallen light renew!

"O Earth, O Earth, return!
Arise from out the dewy grass;
    Night is worn,
    And the morn
Rises from the slumberous mass.

"Turn away no more;
Why wilt thou turn away?
    The starry floor,
    The wat'ry shore,
Is giv'n thee till the break of day." '